W9-CBE-455

s w i m m e r

Swimmer is a striking, supple and direct novel from an exciting new British writer. It tells the story of a girl who, having hidden from the confusions of childhood first in dreams of flying and then by falling in love with water, is subsequently coached to become a successful international athlete.

But when a child has wished for the world – and got it – who or what can help her plot a course through the deeper, darker waters that lie beyond the training pool, out there in Real Life?

Lyrical, moving, perfectly achieved, *Swimmer* is a simply staggering debut.

SWIMMER

BILL BROADY

Flamingo
An Imprint of HarperCollins*Publishers*

Flamingo
an imprint of HarperCollins*Publishers*
77–85 Fulham Palace Road,
Hammersmith, London W6 8JB

www.fireandwater.com

Published by Flamingo 2000
1 3 5 7 9 8 6 4 2

Copyright © Bill Broady 2000

Bill Broady asserts the moral right to
be identified as the author of this work

This novel is entirely a work of fiction.
The names, characters and incidents
portrayed in it are the work of the author's
imagination. Any resemblance to actual persons, living or dead,
events or localities is entirely coincidental.

A catalogue record for this book
is available from the British Library

Photograph of Bill Broady © Charlie Meecham 1999
Endpaper shows a detail of 'The Entomologist's Dream' from
Le Papillon Rouge by Edmund Dulac, 1909.
Courtesy of the Trustees of the V&A

ISBN 0 00 225946 X

Set in Postscript Linotype Sabon
Typeset by Rowland Phototypesetting Ltd,
Bury St Edmunds, Suffolk

Printed and bound in Great Britain by
Clays Ltd, St Ives plc

All rights reserved. No part of this publication may be
reproduced, stored in a retrieval system, or transmitted,
in any form or by any means, electronic, mechanical,
photocopying, recording or otherwise, without the prior
permission of the publishers.

Apparent rari nantes in gurgite vasto

VIRGIL: AENEID 1, line 118

Here and there in the wastes of ocean a swimmer was seen

I

YOUR FIRST AND LAST MEMORIES were of butterflies . . .

. . . Of watching the Red Admiral as it tracked patches of watery sunshine across the garden. It was like an illustration from one of Dad's books, animated – too beautiful to be alive. Vivid and gay but serene, silent: what you had taken for the sound of its wings was the beating of your own heart. You could feel its flutterings on your nerve ends.

Before Dad's identification you'd named it already, in the fast-receding synaesthetic language of babyhood, MRRLYMBRXBRX. You called, and for a moment it rested on your knee, so light that you felt no tickle of contact, its wing-rows of unblinking black eyes looking back into yours.

Then, with a sudden urgent resolve, it began to rise in a tightening spiral until, seeming to pierce the flat grey clouds, it disappeared.

'Where has it gone?' you wailed.

Mum sighed: 'Heaven, I suppose.'

Dad said something about preferring moths, but you hated those diamond-faceted eyes, the nightly sound of their hairy bellies slapping on your windowpane. They went away if you turned out the lights but you were too afraid of the dark: if one ever touched you you'd die – 'Kill not the moth or butterfly,' said Dad, 'for the last judgement draweth nigh.'

You used to scream a lot, especially when plucked from your long-cooled bath. Your feet thudded against Mum's chest: shutting your eyes, it seemed, no longer made you invisible.

'She's a bad girl!'

'No,' said Dad, 'she's a mermaid, a nixie.'

It wasn't the water itself that you loved, more that the feeling of suspension gave you some illusion of flight – like when you'd clutched your birthday kite, a tiger-fanged

Chinese demon, before a Primrose Hill wind twitched its string from your mittened hands and bore it down into the hazy silver city.

At Worthing, aged five, you learned to swim. Dad had left you on the beach, to seek inland the graves of famous writers: Mum took off her belt and tied it around your waist, then grimly led you to the sea. For a moment you were scared – the water seethed and pummeled at you like tiny indignant fists – then realized that it was all in play, that this new, white world was welcoming you, that these whispers and roars were a language you understood, that the tides beat with the same pulse as your circulating blood, that you were not so much discovering as returning.

You splashed, swam, flew. When Dad returned you no longer needed towing: 'We should have called her Woglinde! Wellgunde! Flosshilde!' Mum looked depressed again, as if things hadn't quite worked out as planned. You edged further and further out, ducking regularly to scry the muddy depths, somehow knowing just how to breathe. Then you surfaced to warning shouts: a huge wave was ahead, like a rushing steel wall . . . but you struck out straight towards it, only to see it part miraculously to let you through – just as well, you thought, otherwise you'd have smashed it to vapour.

By the end of the week you had two distinct strokes: Dad's thrashing 'Not Drowning But Waving' style, and Mum's stately crawl. On the way home, Dad stopped the limping hire car to picnic on the Downs: as you lay on your tummy eating crab and cress sandwiches you realized that your legs were still automatically scissoring away. Suddenly you were enveloped by a mass of tiny, pale blue butterflies: it was as if the sky had exploded and all its pieces were now floating gently down.

'*Lysandra coridon poda*,' said Dad. 'The Chalkhill Blues. Here for the horseshoe vetch.'

'He knows everything about everything,' said Mum, 'and it's never got him anywhere.'

Dad assumed a silly German accent to quote his particular hero, that philosopher with a name like a sneeze: 'To me, the butterflies and soap-bubbles and whatever is like them amongst us seem most to enjoy happiness.' On the back of his white shirt the Chalkhill Blues were forming regular lozenge-shaped patterns: you thought you could hear them giggling but then realized that it was you.

When you got home you went straight upstairs and jumped out of the window. Still filled with the butterflies' lightness you didn't even bother to flap your arms, but you must have had some intimation of failure because you cleared the soaps and shampoos from the bathroom sill so as to fall on to the merciful softness of Mum's precious zinnias and not the concrete under your bedroom.

'You don't need to fly –' Dad was holding you unhurt in his arms ' – that's what your imagination's for!' Mum stared in silence at the ruined flowers.

You began to live for the swimming pool. You'd always been awkward, always falling over, into or through things and supposedly inanimate objects went out of their way to cut and bruise you, but now that you'd found a truer element you felt like one of those gods that Dad talked about, who assumed human form to walk the earth. It was as if a sedulous shell fulfilled all school and family commitments, while your essence remained behind, safely submerged. The water was always different: warm or freezing, choppy or calm, technicolour blue-green or yellow and sudsy like in the washing-up bowl, as if the pool had its own unpredictable weather, its independent seasons. The chlorine smell was somehow reassuring, reminding you of Mum's breath. Even so, every time you dived in – the classic spear entry came naturally to you – there was the vestigial hope that you might just hover, then ascend, slipping through the roof's retracted skylight and up into the blue, so that when you did hit the water it was always – much as you loved it – a slight disappointment. Increasingly bored with your classmates' surface noise and bustle, you'd sink to the bottom and just stand watching your air bubbles turning into tiny fish and sea horses and the eddies making your butterfly bracelet seem to flutter and grow.

One afternoon a strange little man was at the poolside, scribbling in a red notebook, watching you. Afterwards your teacher led him over: she said he was The Coach. He pushed and pulled, hefted and lifted you – as if he were contemplating eating you. He was covered in hair: yellow, orange, red and white gradations on his head, face covered with black dots and spines, ear lobes fluffed like dandelions, nostrils tamped with dark shag like Dad's pipe. He tugged your ponytail, bent your ankles – 'High plantar flexion,' he said – then, pressing his brown paws on to your shoulders, looking hard into your eyes: 'A butterfly, I think' . . . Later, when the changing-room had emptied, you went to the mirror and, contorting yourself, sought your nascent wings.

'Strength! Stamina! Suppleness!' Coach was shouting. He swore by The Three Ss, The Ten Dos and Ten Don'ts, The Cycle Of Learning, The Golden Rule and The Big No-No. Your arm-entry points might have been perfect, your dive angle shallow, your undulation minimal, but it still hurt. Hamstring, sartorius, gracilis, psoas: muscles you didn't know you had introduced themselves through pain. Butterfly wasn't an elegant floating but a desperate thrashing: not the stroke you'd dreamed of, by which you'd be carried in the direction and at the speed desired with no more exertion than a thought. Coach was making you force the water to do what it was willing to do anyway: it was as if he'd stuck boxing gloves on your hands and thrust you into a ring with your best friend.

Not that you had a best friend. Or a worst enemy – or indeed any particular intimacies or antipathies. For some reason you were made to spend your days among children: you watched them in the playground – their massings, alliances and sunderings, as if they were being blown about by winds you couldn't feel. They seemed to be a different species, like the things that Dad sometimes showed you through his microscope – alien, though no doubt in some obscure way necessary. Your breathing sounded like a steam engine but theirs was imperceptible, their chests remaining as stiff as the walls. You thought of one of Mum's favourite sayings, 'Most people don't even know they've been born,' and saw your classmates – amorphous, diffuse, floating – as foetuses still. They radiated smugness, serene in their amniotic fluid of months, years, lifetimes, while you had only minutes, seconds, fractions of seconds. Life for them was an endless stream, but for you it had become a succession of countdowns: Coach's stopwatch had atomized time. The girl next to you in class did nothing but sit and stare, stare and sit: you could have swum two lengths in the time it took her to retie her sandal-straps. Whenever you spoke to anyone they'd blush and stammer, part-frightened, part-thrilled, as if you'd been a talking tree or bird. Your teacher told Dad that the whole school had a crush on you, but you weren't flattered: you imagined them advancing in a phalanx to flatten and smother you.

You never thought of yourself as being a child. When you made the Regional Junior Squad, now a four-stroke swimmer, you binned your one-eared teddy bear, Buddenbrooks – so-called because he resembled another of Dad's favourites, Thomas Mann. You dropped ballet. Coach said, 'We can't let her arms run behind her legs. Kangaroos can't swim.'

'It's art, not callisthenics,' said Dad, but the piano lessons had to go too, though not before he'd speculated about getting a Bechstein to float.

'Strength! Stamina! Suppleness!' . . . 'Stupidity! Stolidity! Senselessness!' – Dad parodied it in his German voice. He was at every practice, squatting precariously on his camp-stool, oblivious to your trouncing everyone at broken sets, never looking up from his poetry, those bewildering snakes and ladders of seemingly unrelated words and letters. The other parents moaned incessantly about their sacrifices of time and money or jumped around yelling threats or encouragement, chiming in with Coach's motivational chants: 'Work to win! Win to work!'

'*Arbeit macht frei*,' observed Dad, finishing the *TLS* cross-word with a flourish. The others called him Mr Stupid, pre-sumably because that was how he made them all feel. You looked at him with a tight, sick feeling, never sure whether you were proud or ashamed.

Training took place first thing in the morning and late evening, before the pool opened to the public and after it closed. School allowed you to miss Prayers and Period One and to sleep through many others. At night you felt you were calming and soothing the water after its ten-hour mauling, as if it were a nervous horse. There was something magical and transgressive about being there, as if you were burglars, spies or ghosts. Reflections danced and shifted on the ceiling like half-visible spirits. The day's laughter, splashings and shouts seemed to have combined in a continuous echo-pattern, like the barking of dogs: when you surfaced you sometimes feared you'd be ringed by snapping, red-eyed curs. You liked the morning sessions best, as the dawn light crept like a flood tide up the walls and the only sound was an unending soft exhalation and the surface was so calm and glassy that your dive's cleaving of it seemed to be a greater miracle than flying.

You felt yourself trading molecules with the water in an ever-deepening intimacy that remained volatile, never easy, never secure. In motion you weren't sure if you were fleeing or in pursuit, swimming towards something or away from it. Sometimes the water was tender, at others it scratched your skin like sand: having caressed you it would suddenly punch you in the gut. One evening, shivering with the flu, nose and eyes streaming, hardly able even to climb on to your block, you found yourself, on entry, completely cured ... but next day, feeling back at full thrust, you were drained after thirty seconds, facing hours of unrelieved agony. Increasingly, though, how you felt made no difference to your times: your muscles had taken over and left your feelings and thoughts and your pain, dissociated, to drift away.

As the endorphins kicked in and you torpedoed up and down the pool you often thought of butterflies – sometimes even keeping an eye out for them, as if they too might have decided to switch their allegiance to water. Whether because of Mum's sprays or global warming they were never to be seen in your garden now. Perhaps you just didn't have the time to watch for them or perhaps they were avoiding you. Finally, if one had appeared you would have been as surprised as if salmon had begun to nest in the poplar tree. In one of your waking moments at school you'd learnt that the Greek word for butterfly was Psyche: it also meant soul. And there had been a butterfly-goddess, too:

Surely I dreamt today, or did I see
The wingèd Psyche with awaken'd eyes?

You loved Keats but never let on to Dad because you knew he loved him too.

One morning at seven you were all gathered at the side of the pool, listening to Coach: 'Do your time, do your time! Don't look at the others. Don't even think about the others. Just do your time, do your time!' He made it sound as if you were prisoners, in for a long stretch, with no parole or pardon. Suddenly there appeared behind him a dirty, bristled man, wearing a corded tartan dressing-gown ... legs wide apart, leaning back so that his head looked heavenwards, he whipped it open. You all dived, screaming, back underwater, as Dad and Coach dragged him away, but you'd glimpsed that there'd been no hair, no . . . winkle between his legs, just a bubble-gum-pink expanse: a flash of nothing.

Competition was the price you had to pay for spending so much time in the water. Not that it was particularly competitive: at local, national and junior international levels you just won and won, absently, without any real pleasure. You didn't like having to turn in races and go back again, as if you'd forgotten something: the 100 metres was only the same 50 twice, the 200, four times. Swimming back through your own wake you always feared that you'd crash into yourself coming the other way. They should have built pools that expanded or contracted to the required length, or huge circular ones in which you'd spiral round until you reached the centre. At the climax of a race your vision would always begin to fog: it was as if you were heading into a shimmering grey light – you'd reach out but it would remain tantalizingly just beyond your hand's final touch on the rail. Even when you won you were disappointed: you'd look at your empty hands and then have to move out for the next race, although you could feel the water trying to hold you there, clinging to your legs like a lonely, desperate child.

You were also guesting with other clubs, hunting wild card invitations to European meets, but Mum and Dad never came to watch you race: it hadn't been discussed, just tacitly understood that you all wanted it that way. Coach and the ASA arranged the transport, accommodation and chaperoning. Dad kept up your cuttings book: in among your triumphant progress he interpolated his own imaginings. There were mocked-up headlines: NORTH LONDON GIRL SWIMS TO THE MOON ... MERMAID SIGHTED NEAR GRAND UNION CANAL – and photomontages of you with a scaly tail, pursued by Neptune in his Triton-drawn chariot, your goggled, strabismic eyes unaware of three breaking shark-fins and Nessie's snaky neck, or receiving your five County medals from a Cranach Venus naked except for her jewels and fur hat ... and your Junior Gold from Karloff's Frankenstein monster.

When you weren't swimming you were exercising or sleeping – at school they taught in whispers so as not to wake you.

Coach had you running, pounding the pavements in a daily bastinado to Somers Town and back: sometimes you'd whirl your arms in the hope that rotoring into the air might give you some relief. You loathed it, but somehow Coach could always tell by looking in your eyes whether you'd skived. '95% isn't enough,' he'd say, '100% isn't enough! . . . Strive! . . . And give me 105! . . . And then . . . give me 110!' He racked and taxed you with dips, pulls, press-ups, burpees, weights. At home you had a twelve-exercise muscle circuit from garage to attic. Yoked like an ox, you'd spend hours in the living room stepping on and off Dad's massive two volumes of Sir William Rothenstein's red-chalk drawings of forgotten '20s celebrities, watching over and over your favourite video, *Love Story*. You silently mouthed Oliver's killer last line to his martinet father: 'Love means never having to say you're sorry.' Dad had known the man who had written it: 'Well, he got his thirty pieces of silver, but he's finished as a serious classical scholar.'

Dad was quieter these days. Sometimes on the cross-London rail journeys to the Crystal Palace Olympic-size pool he'd sit staring into his book, but the page would never turn and his eyes would flicker as if the words were dancing around. As you waited for the last Northern Line back from Waterloo two coppers always hassled you. 'Excuse me, sir . . . Is this your . . . daughter?' You'd watch the departure board stuck at NEXT TRAIN: HIGH BARNET – 1 MINUTE for a quarter of an hour as they flicked the ends of your wet hair, brushed against your hips and bottom or just stood looking at you with burning eyes. You'd pray that a drunk or a black man would appear to draw them away. Dad used to ask, 'Why is there never a criminal around when you need one?' Your faith in him had recently been seriously shaken by the welkin. It was what he called water, the sea, and you'd adopted it because of its resonances of health and close affinity, but when you looked it up in his *OED* you found that it actually meant the sky.

At fourteen you graduated to the senior squad. Coach wangled you a sports scholarship to the public school where he was co-ordinator of games, but there were still the fees to be found. Dad took on extra work: stuffing envelopes at the Church Commissioners', cramming Japanese students for Goldsmith's and, for three months, doing the night shift at a petrol station. 'It's the first proper job I've ever had,' he joked. He'd sit watching the weird shadows flitting across the rainbow grease, his fingers shifting on the baseball bat they'd given him, as if on the keys of his beloved Conn tenor saxophone, long gone into hock.

'All these sacrifices,' said Mum. 'All that money. And for what?'

'For nothing,' Dad laughed. 'That's the point of sport: it's pointless. A glorious waste of time – though not quite as glorious or as pointless as art.'

Mum lit another cigarette, like a holed, pursued battleship putting out smoke camouflage. You wondered how anyone could think that being the best in the country or even the world was pointless, for nothing. Finally the oil company sponsored you for the rest of the money. 'I've been bought off,' said Dad, rather sadly. With his beard and big books he'd apparently been scaring away not only the robbers but the customers: they thought he was a black magician.

The new school stood at a confluence of howling Northern winds, large and black like Castle Dracula, but shored up with strutted white-wood CLASP extensions which led to silos containing an athletics track, squash and tennis courts and a fifty-metre pool. The moorland birds didn't sing, just rattled or shrieked their alarms, and there were no butterflies among the burnt heather stubs and gorse, only – in summer – fat and unnaturally aggressive bees. At least the girls here didn't moon about but got on with things – somersaulting, swimming, running – but they had an alarmingly mechanical quality, their arms and legs appearing to be jointed like dolls, their glassy eyes rattling and rolling in their sockets. 'Send in the clones,' observed Dad on his only visit. He too had noticed that they all had the same permanent, infolding smile: 'Like the Mona Lisa crossed with the Thurber hippopotamus that has just eaten Dr Millmoss.' These girls' only crushes were on themselves.

It was like a prison or a monastery: an edgy sodality with its impenetrable private language – swimmers' argot, backslung TV catch phrases and an endless roll of nicknames. Tooting, Cheesy, Shaky, Claret . . . some girls had dozens but you had just these four. You used to get purple-faced after you'd been training flat out – hence beetrooting, through rooting to Tooting; then you'd puke bile and the colour would fade to leave on your skin white lumps like cottage cheese, hence Cheesy; and then you'd tremble uncontrollably for a few minutes, hence Shaky – they used to hum Shakin' Stevens' 'This Old House' when you walked into the dining room. Claret was because your nose often bled when you got really excited, especially during the wait for a relay changeover . . .

But there was also a fifth name, the one you weren't quite meant to hear: at first you thought with a shock that it was 'Psyche' they were whispering, but then realized that the moniker that your silences, tempers and hard elbow-points had earned you was Psycho.

The other girls needed to highlight such flaws in order to live with the irritating but ineluctable fact of your beauty. You were the one they always used for the training films, for the posters, manuals and brochures. You even looked good modelling the national team uniform: the skirt's stiffness somehow folded into sunray pleats, the clumpy shoe-heels lengthened and narrowed, even the awful ribboned straw hat seemed chic, its brim following a salty downward curve until, as if caroming off your left eyebrow, it ascended, just kissing the top of your ear en route to infinity. For hours in front of their mirrors the others sought in vain to achieve that perfect angle until forced to concede what they'd suspected all along – that what had been perfect was you. 'The Botticellian Butter-fly', one newspaper styled you: set among simple heartiness you looked poignantly inappropriate – embodying delicacy not strength, suppleness not power, your pallor affirming above youth and health some terminal but romantic malady. Your expression was always solemn, even when smiling, but your body always appeared to be well-pleased with itself.

In the school, Karen was your one close friend – or, at least, the only other girl who, while not being a misfit or a rebel, was also somehow tangential. She had suddenly emerged from nowhere – well, from Yorkshire – as your main butterfly rival. Having finished second to you in the Nationals, she was now beginning to overhaul you in practice. If you didn't care about winning you now discovered that you also hated to lose. Karen was painfully shy, permanently blushing, always ducking her head to avoid eye contact. You loved her gentle voice but she never said much, except once when she tried to get you to teach her how to 'speak properly' – your North London accent sounded positively regal to her. You spent countless hours back to back on the SCR sofa, snoozing and listening to Nik Kershaw's *The Riddle* again and again – you never did work out what it was all about.

One day, after practice, she told you that Jesus Christ – complete with beard, crown of thorns, pierced hands, feet and side and a sorrowful, all-knowing, all-forgiving look – had been swimming alongside her in the next lane. He'd been doing only a sort of fast dog paddle, but had managed to keep up with her OK. He was trying to tell her how she could swim through her own body and out into the realm of pure spirit . . . but she said that she hadn't been able to hear him properly for all his splashing about.

Jesus didn't come back, but Karen began to sing hymns in the shower, then shaved her head and starved and flagellated herself. 'All butterflies are crazy, like goalkeepers,' said Coach. 'It must do something to the brain.' They took her away from school, but you didn't understand why they also felt it necessary to drop her from the team – through it all, her times had been unaffected. Although you did miss her you also felt a certain relief: you breezed the next Nationals at both distances. Sometimes you worried that her madness might have been contagious. To swim out of your body into pure spirit: in those final metres when exhaustion set in and the grey haze descended, you felt as if you might have known all too well what Karen – or Christ – had meant.

The world – as Coach liked to say – was your lobster. You could confirm that all major countries had airports, streets with people and cars, and interchangeable hotels with beds of varying discomfort. And the water was always wet – although some of the pools in Mediterranean countries did have moss or mould growing up the sides. In Spain it was so turbid as to appear bottomless: Coach claimed to have glimpsed the masts and funnels of sunken ships. Your winning grab for the rail nearly broke your wrist: afterwards, measuring the pool, you found it to be twelve centimetres short. 'Spanish metres must be different,' said Coach. The water behind the Iron Curtain was always ice-cold, with a rusty taste, as if it had been long-stored in cans. Once, in Prague, something stabbed into your push-off foot on the first turn: pain and shock goaded you into frantic activity. On the third lap you realized that you were swimming back through a rose-pink cloud of your own blood. Desperate, you exploded again, to record your fastest-ever time. When they checked the wall there was no apparent cause: you suspected Coach, who had often speculated about deploying blowpipes or cattle-prods. Doc blinked at the inch-long spine he'd tweez-ered out of your sole: 'Medical science confesses itself baffled,' he said, 'unless a porcupine was passing by.' Afterwards, the Czechs presented you with a massive medal of dark wood like a cask-lid, carved with a strange animal – half-bear, half-chicken. 'It's a nice place to visit,' said Coach, as he did about everywhere, 'but I wouldn't want to live here.'

In the Europeans you finished fourth, behind two stubbled, steroided East German hulks and a cork-skinned Russian who, pre-race, had been pumped full of oxygen-rich new blood. They snarled at you as if they'd only taken the drugs as a handicap and felt that you were cheating by not cheating. You knew that with an effective testing system you'd have had the gold and, for your subsequent fifth and sixth in the Olympics and World Championships, silver and bronze. 'You're just unlucky,' sighed Coach, 'in a few years' time we'll be able to do it, too.' Remembering the Russian girl's face – blank-eyed, drooling – you didn't feel particularly deprived.

At least you'd always done your time, done your time – indeed, you usually improved on it, so that you were regularly defeating yourself. What you really loved was setting records – no, breaking records, smashing them. You had a mental picture of a hovering vinyl round – some music you hated like 'This Old House', Joe Dolce's 'Shaddup You Face', or Dad's booming Wagner or Slim'n'Slam 78s – a big black shiny zero that was blotting out the sun . . . which suddenly exploded into flying shards and grey dust, as if hit by a sniper's bullet, allowing the light to come flooding through.

At the end of the competitive season the other squad members would fall into heavy, silent depressions, but you were secretly pleased at being able to resume unmediated contact with the water. While they hibernated you embarked on prodigious long-distance swimming programmes. Coach, fearing that you'd lose your edge, was always trying to stop you. 'You need your speed! Need your speed!' he kept saying, but to no avail. Fifty miles in twenty-four hours: another disk – the British Endurance record – went smithereening. You were the queen of the Charity Swimathon: most of the Navy had sponsored you at a pound a mile – afterwards they sent

a telegram: YOU'VE BANKRUPTED THE FLEET BUT THE
FLEET STILL LOVES YOU ANYWAY. They helicoptered you
out to an aircraft-carrier for the admiral to present you with
a door-sized cardboard cheque. Then the sailors three-cheered
you and bore you round in triumph. Even though you felt your
swimsuit ride right up at the back, there were no comments or
wandering hands – they looked at you without lust, with a
sort of bashful reverence. Perhaps all the best men joined the
Navy: or was it that the sea's lulling rhythms had taught them
kindness and love? After they'd piped you away you looked
back, eyes misting, to see the deck a fluttering mass of white
caps, waving.

Coach was at the centre of your world. Despite his sloganiz-
ing, sulks and foot-stampings, you all loved him. He knew
just when to pressurize and when to slacken off, whether to
threaten or cajole. And he was always fun: sometimes you'd
slap his spreading pink tonsure, with a sound like a fish hitting
a marble slab, and he'd chase you, growling like a bear, flick-
ing at your legs with his blackboard pointer. You knew he
was just a big softy by the way he draped his arm around
your neck, massaged the stiffness out of your shoulders, gently

squeezed your forearm at the end of a really gruelling session. And when you won – or even did your time – he'd hug you so hard that you'd feel you might go right through him and out the other side . . . and weren't those tears in his eyes? Dad had strangely stiffened up around your twelfth birthday – no more kisses or sitting on his knee – as if you'd committed some unforgivable crime. On visits home you felt as if you were shrinking, getting colder and colder: Mum's lap looked as distant and unattainable as Mount Everest. The school doctor had put you on the Pill to regularize your periods for competitions: when Mum found the packet she slapped your face and then, having listened to your tearful explanations, nodded and slapped you again.

In fact, you hardly ever got to see any boys. At meets and championships the only real interaction between Men's and Women's teams was a series of practical jokes: your face ached from trying to laugh with everyone else at the apple-pie beds, fire-extinguisher fights or purloined underwear. The male star – your equivalent – was impossibly gangling, ichthycephalic with patchy, lemonish tufts of hair, sandy lashes under thick black brows and eyes that seemed confused and unfocused, like something unborn. Racked by self-consciousness, he hid his raw and acned face, peeling and flaking, behind the ramparts of an upturned batwing collar. At the poolside, stripped, his head would roll into his shoulder like Quasimodo's, attempting at least to conceal half of his shame. But this was the very thing that you liked about him: the red and gold whorls and rosettes on his grey body made him appear to be in mid-metamorphosis, as if – especially in the patches around his large-areolated nipples and inner thighs – they were forming scales. His name was Tom, the same as the transfigured little sweep in *The Water Babies*, but you thought of him as The Merman. You knew when he was about to enter the room: a gentle wind seemed to pass across your face. In your dreams you were swimming together, skin to skin, merging. Your eyes never met, you never spoke to each other, but once, at a post-competition disco, your team-mates, sniggering, pushed you together on the dancefloor: 'Beauty and The Beast'! You danced to one of your favourite records, Steve Arrington's 'Feel (So Real)': Tom's head was twisting round so far that it almost faced in the wrong direction. You put one hand, then the other on his shoulders – they were ridged, and solid as rock – before you felt the blood from your nose dripping on to your bare feet and you bolted back to your respective groups. You told Mum about him: 'The shy boys,' she said, with a glare at Dad, 'are always the sly boys.' Coach just put his arms in the teapot position, flared his nostrils like Kenneth Williams and lisped: 'A little bit that way, I'm afraid, our Thomas.'

On the last day of the Europeans, the night of your sixteenth birthday, you lost what Mum had always called Your Jewel. You'd got properly drunk for the first time, after an evening of party games – Up Jenkyns!, Dumb Crambo, Animal & Stick – spiced with Draconian booze forfeits. Coach helped you to your room, then kissed you, his tongue exploring your teeth and gums like a slow-crawling snail, and you realized with a rancid choke that the characteristic smell on Mum's breath was the same as his – gin. He began twiddling your nipples, as if trying to fine-tune a radio to a fading signal: as he loosened your clothing and precisely arranged your limbs you wondered if you were moving on to a new section of Buck Dawson's 'Dry Land Exercises'. 'I've been waiting eight years for this moment,' said Coach. You couldn't recall much of what happened next: he chose to interpret your lapses into unconsciousness as signs of excess ecstasy – likewise, presumably, your vomiting. Next morning he was grumpy and suspicious because you hadn't bled: you nearly replied that you only did that when you got excited. He insisted on photographing you, naked and shivering, on the Latissimus Machine. It never occurred to you to report him, but you did wonder where the usually eagle-eyed chaperones had been during all this. You didn't feel particularly different: just slightly heavier in the pool, as if you were shipping a little more water, and for a few days you had a strange sensation of cobwebs brushing your face. When Coach did try again, back at school, it was without much enthusiasm: he seemed almost relieved when you pushed him away – being the first was all he had really cared about.

'Being first is what matters,' said Coach. 'Records will always be broken, but a medal is forever, is history.' The Commonwealth Games were coming up again: the last remnant of Empire, of colonialism and imperialism – the final redoubt of sportsmanship and fair play. Now that you had a real chance of a silver – maybe even a gold – just doing your time, doing your time was suddenly no longer enough. It was now that Coach called on his full motivational skills: he gave you photographs of your main rivals and made you deface their fresh, smiling faces with felt-penned duelling scars and large Pierrot-style teardrops. At the last practice, an ASA bigwig with a white moustache appeared and gave an interminable speech which ended, 'It's the spirit of the thing that counts: it's not the winning but the taking part.'

'You heard the nice man,' said Coach afterwards, 'it's not the winning it's the taking apart . . . the old fart!'

Back in London for a week you were quite unable to follow Coach's instructions to taper – to stay out of the water, storing up extra energy for release on the day. 'You need your speed! Need your speed!' – but you were as hooked on your weekly 75,000 metres as Mum was on her hourly toper's visits to the bathroom. During this stay you discovered her bottle of Gordon's floating inside the toilet cistern. Disguised in an old swim-cap, you sneaked into small pools where no one knew you: being back in the water with normal people again was like swimming through a lunatic asylum. You even tried the Ladies' Pond at Kenwood, but a short-haired woman smiled at you and called you 'sister' so you fled in mortal fear of sapphism. 'Bad news,' said Dad, as you came in, 'Russia and the GDR have just applied to join the Commonwealth.': your heart sank before you realized he was joking, although he hadn't smiled.

The Commonwealth Games were always the best one, the most relaxed – being only a Grade B terrorist target. On the first morning, while your team-mates were having fun throwing furniture into the practice pool then fishing it out again, you dodged the chaperones and wandered away from the Games Village. Although London born and bred it was as if you'd never seen a city before: turning left-right-left-right, you cut across the streams of machines and people, through the heat-shimmering air, under a blue-black sky – the welkin! – that seemed to balance on the tops of the tallest buildings like a precarious lid. The hairs in your nose tickled, you felt light-headed with being alone for once – half-lost, free.

Just when you'd begun to feel tired, a small park presented itself. After buying a sandwich and a styrofoam coffee at a stall by the gate you sat down on grass that was thick, clean and dry like grown-out Astroturf. At its centre was the statue of a standing figure, gesturing with an extravagantly-plumed hat, his expression at once awestruck and proprietorial. You didn't recognize the name but you knew he must have been the man who had discovered this park. It was the best sandwich you'd ever eaten: some sort of diced sausage, hard and salty, with something sourish – olives? – something sweet – capsicum? – and the distinctive metallic tang of watercress. Its crisp top was studded with unfamiliar seeds and husks. When you opened it up, however, the inside looked so revolting – a viscous smear of colours – that you couldn't face another mouthful.

The park was full of young office workers on their lunch breaks. They'd formed two large groups, one poring over a newspaper crossword, the other devoted to what appeared to be a glitteringly choreographed mass flirtation. Eyes sparkled and teeth gleamed in their tanned faces: the vivid floral designs on the girls' dresses were echoed by the men's ties. There was one boy who wasn't smiling, who sat slightly apart from the others. He was watching you, his chin resting on his knees: you moved to tug down your skirt hem but then didn't bother. You lay on your back, then rolled over. Although every flower petal in front of you remained in sharp focus, the whole parterre was shifting in the heat like a kaleidoscope. It was as if, after many years adrift, you'd finally been cast up on a friendly shore. All you wanted was for the Chalkhill Blues to descend, but five thousand miles was too far for them to fly.

Then there was a high, shrill sound: all the workers had linked arms and were marching out of the park, whistling the Seven Dwarves' Hi-Ho-Hi-Ho song. Dad always called offices 'Concentration camps of the soul', but you watched them go as if they were the gods returning to Valhalla over the Rainbow Bridge. The serious boy looked back once. You imagined their destination: an office full of lovers, light-heartedly but seriously doing mysterious but important things with computers – things to do with charity, fashion or the news.

In the last school production you'd played Miranda in *The Tempest*: now you recalled one of the bits for which you hadn't needed the prompt:

> O *wonder*
> *How many goodly creatures are there here!*
> *How beauteous mankind is! O brave new world*
> *That has such people in't!*

You felt that this moment marked the end of your childhood and the start of the rest of your life, that with these Games the water ended and the land began – but you weren't afraid, for you knew that this brave new world would be your lobster. The park was quiet now, empty apart from a tramp in the bushes: all you could see of him was a pair of bare feet and three bottles – two emptied, the other half-full of purple. You were afraid he might be dead, but then noticed that the filthy toes were wiggling in the sunlight. On such a day, everything was pleasing, everyone was pleased . . . When, taking alternate rights and lefts, you had reluctantly made your way back to the village you found it echoing with police sirens: your disappearance had given them the excuse for a Full Red Security Alert.

Things did not go well in the pool: you only just scraped through the heats. Energy surges alternated with waves of fatigue so that you progressed in a series of jolts. The water felt indifferent and inert, neither helping nor hindering. You couldn't stop thinking about the boy in the park: you'd already forgotten his face, but that didn't matter – you gave him a thousand new ones. Strangely, you never once thought about going back to look for him.

Coach kept raging about your not having tapered, about the sunburn you'd got on that first day, but he obviously suspected something more. You saw him going through your bag in the changing-room: was he looking for drugs? – incriminating diary entries? – a local telephone number? You finished third in the slower semi. Blanking out Coach's increasingly desperate slogans you merely muttered that you were saving yourself for the final, but you both knew that you'd only ever had two speeds – flat out and stationary, all or nothing.

On the morning of the race you went through the usual rituals: Coach produced his cutthroat razor – chuckling and making it flicker menacingly in the light – and shaved down your arms and legs and that narrow but persistent ladder of golden hair ascending from mid-spine to nape. 'The future is a straight line,' he intoned, 'the future is a straight line.' You were afraid he'd cut you as you shook with suppressed laughter. He cleaned your aura – running his hands round your body's contours half an inch away and then shaking his fingers vigorously – he claimed they felt as if they were covered with a sticky dough. 'The future is a straight line': he kept it up all the way to the poolside – you feared that you'd be too weak from giggling to be able to swim at all.

You stood behind your block and took a deep breath, then, closing your eyes, offered up your usual pre-race prayer. As always a dark butterfly-like shape passed across the red field of your eyelids as you whispered: 'Almighty God, please help me to do my best and give me strength. And keep my nose from bleeding. For ever and ever, Amen.' Exhaling, you opened your eyes and moved forward. You knew, of course, that all the other girls would be doing the same thing and that God couldn't be everybody's ace-in-the-hole – unless there were as many gods as there were swimmers.

The favourite was in the next lane: a Canadian girl with olive skin that seemed to be holding water in suspension on its surface – an unfair advantage, you'd always felt. You hardly recognized her without the blackened-out teeth and eye-patch you'd been forced to add to her photograph. Her fingernails were varnished a bright silver and she appeared, curiously, to be wearing heavy make-up. She smiled at you and spoke:

'Butterflies.' She brought her hands together with a fluttering motion. You just stared. 'I'm full of them,' she said, rolling her great dark eyes and clapping her palms loudly against her flat stomach. You realized that she was only talking about nerves, but it so confused you that you forgot to do your usual steadying count of the lane-flags. Swimmers weren't even supposed to look at each other, let alone talk, before a race: she'd been trying – literally – to psych you out.

You threw yourself at the water as if it were the Canadian's throat: anger gave you a massive hang and carry, like coming off the topmost board. After the entry and glide you seemed to be fully half-way down before you started the stroke – great retributive arm-sweeps, like Godzilla levelling a city. You swam with an aggression you hadn't felt since you'd faced down that great wave off Worthing – you pulverized the water, smashed it. All style and smoothness were lost: your breathing was so ragged that you felt you'd gulped down a considerable volume of the pool, like a whale. You made the first turn so fast that you felt your body morphing, leaving your scrambled atoms desperately recombining . . . and you felt somehow ashamed, as if you'd abused the water's trust, as if it had been an evil length you'd just swum.

Now came the retribution as the water, dark and vengeful, closed and wrestled with you. Although you tried to apologize, it just wasn't biddable. It was all that Canadian cow's fault: you glanced right, expecting to see a swimming Friesian, with painted face and silver horns and hooves, its udders swinging in the undertow. Jabbing with a thousand hard fingers, the water enwrapped you, not slowing you but sweeping you away, forcing you to go ever faster, faster than anyone could bear. Then it was as if you'd gone over the edge of a cataract . . . you were in free fall, until your instinctively outstretched palms hit the rail with a bone-jarring impact – as you pushed off again you were sure that you could feel the perspex cracking under the soles of your feet.

After the turn you found that you were looking into the silvery-grey shimmer – the warning marker for the end of your tether – a full eighty metres too soon. How could you even finish? Would you drown or just come to pieces in the water? And this time it didn't teasingly recede as usual but held its position, allowing you to swim right into it.

Then you were floating, almost motionless, as if in the doldrums: without your arms' continued thrashing you felt you would have been borne backwards. Banks of mist rolled in: were you imagining, on its condensed surface, the faint mirror image of your own goggled face? This could only be one place: you had breached the realm of pure spirit. Nothing – neither Christ nor Karen, neither the Canadian cow nor The Flying Dutchman – could be seen in the adjoining lanes. There was dead silence: you couldn't even hear your own breathing. Were you still visible to the crowd? Perhaps you'd be remembered as the swimmer who disappeared – as a cautionary tale of a naughty girl who wouldn't taper and spent so much time in the water that one day she just dissolved. You felt the temptation to linger here forever, having deeper and deeper insights into the nature of pure spirit or fog, but Coach's words suddenly rang in your ears: 'A nice place to visit but I wouldn't want to live here.' Then you had a strange sense of weightlessness: not of flight but of levitation, as if you were being borne upwards out of some great depth, until you were back on the surface, watching your hand reach out to touch the wall, with everything sharp and clear again. You had no idea of your time or placing: for all you knew everyone else had long since finished and gone home, forgetting all about you – maybe you had a chance in the next race or the next championship? You turned for the last time but now with terrible slowness: every muscle protested as you twisted and flexed – the pain hit you.

'No pain, no gain,' Coach liked to say – but this was something different from the customary twinges and stabs. It was somehow external in origin, as if your entire body was adapting to an unfamiliar fifth element, no longer moving through water but through pain. Then the sound hit you. Previously you'd only been dimly aware of the crowd's noise: it had always seemed unrelated – like distant watchdogs barking at shadows – but now you felt that for the first time it really meant something. The whole world sounded to be cheering you on. Although you knew that Mum and Dad were still at home, you were sure that you could distinguish their voices – but as you'd never heard them before, in wordless howls of pride and joy. Coach and the rest of the squad were chanting 'The Future is a Straight Line!' – well, maybe it was? – and Tom's voice wasn't a camp whine but thrilling as a trumpet-blast. You could hear Karen's Yorkshire accent confidently ringing out . . . and the playground hubbub of those poor kids who'd had crushes on you . . . and the boy from the park – smiling at last, his lips drawing away from his teeth with a sharp click.

They sounded like the starving garrison of a besieged fort suddenly sighting an outrider from the relief column. You felt as if you were swimming to save them, to make everything all right for everybody. Swimming for Dad to let you sit on his knee again, for Mum to pour her gin away, for Tom to kiss you and for Coach not to, for Karen to be well again, for Waterloo Station to be cleared of police and thieves. It wasn't, like Dad had said, 'all for nothing', but for everything, for everyone. You suddenly thought of the other swimmers in the race: you felt that they were no longer in contention but instead adding their strength to yours. It was like a magical rite, a pooling of energy and feeling in a single physical act, to cut all the tangled knots, to render the complicated simple once more. 'Do your time! Do your time!' – you seemed to hear, but this time wasn't yours any more: you were sharing it with the other seven and with everyone else on earth. It was as if for a few seconds you were fused with all the people who were being born or dying, killing or making love, working or just idly watching some swimming match on the TV . . . the horizontal became vertical and you flew in a wild spiral, your body shaking as if it were about to break apart. And just as you touched to finish it struck you that this pain wasn't a fifth element, but the thing that somehow held all the others together, that pumped your blood, set the tides, kept the stars in their courses – and that another name for it was love.

You looked to the right and saw a silver-nailed hand grabbing the rail, then holding and twisting in an instant of fury. The water on the left remained clear and calm for a second before the rest of the field, arriving in a body, shattered it. Then the Canadian girl was in your lane, kissing your tearful, bloody face. 'Looks like I wore the wrong varnish' – she grinned and held up a hand. Then half the team dived into the pool, dragging you out as a robotic voice echoed: 'In a new UK and Commonwealth Record'. They chaired you, chanting your name – 'Psy-cho! Psy-cho!' – and you no longer minded, only laughed. 'Second fastest time ever!' screamed Coach. 'You swam out of your skin, girl! Out of your skin!' On the contrary, you thought, you'd just swum back into it.

All the other defeated swimmers and their camps seemed to be genuinely delighted for you: the crowd wouldn't stop cheering – there was no home-town disappointment, unlike in Russia or the States, where even the smallest loss seemed to negate a thousand victories. It was as if it didn't matter who won: you were all part of the same thing, the Common Wealth.

Then you were bowing your head: a gold medal was hung around your neck and your arms were loaded with flowers the names of which you didn't know. A tinny, vaguely familiar sound came from the Tannoy: *God Save the Queen.* The flag was being jerked upwards, a limp cluster of red, white and blue: when it reached the top of the staff it began to twitch, then unfurled itself to flutter bravely, as if the music were belling it out. Godsaveourgraciousqueen: you suddenly realized that you couldn't remember the words of the anthem. The Press had demonized Daley Thompson for whistling and blowing kisses while it played and so, knowing that the cameras were coming in close and that screens all over the world would be filled by your face, you mouthed it a few words behind, hoping that it would look like a satellite delay.

Sendhervictorious ... happyandglorious ... longtoreign-
overus ... it sounded like a register of dinosaurs. You were
struggling not to laugh: the Canadian was tickling your bum
with her bouquet. When you finally stepped off the rostrum
you felt as if you were having to force your feet to remain on
the ground: if you were to fly out of the stadium you feared
that you might be disqualified under some species rule. Coach
shook your hand with a sudden formality: 'If anyone ever
asks you what it was all for,' he said, 'just show them
that medal.' He looked hard into your eyes: 'What the
hell were you doing on that third length? Did you miscount
or what?'

Later, soaking in the bath, you had the odd feeling that
although the taps were off its level was steadily rising. And
this foreign water seemed to be unusually peaty – rufous and
darkening towards plum ... It was blood: your hands went
to your nose, then to between your legs, coming away black
and sticky as you started to scream. The haemorrhage lasted
for about twenty minutes and then stopped. There was no
lesion, it wasn't your period – 'Medical science,' said Doc,
'confesses itself baffled. Unless a porcupine was passing by.'

You felt that in the efforts of that afternoon your virginity had been fully, finally lost.

Doc cleared you for the medley relays: in fact, you felt fitter than ever, as if your system had purged itself of excess or infected blood. Now, even in qualifying, your third leg times had been as fast as in the individual event. In the final you were next to the Canadian again. She didn't speak this time, just winked and fluttered her hands, her newly-gilded fingernails flashing as you waited for the changeover. At the end of the breaststroke leg you were second to the Australians, with Canada a close third. You produced another of your huge dives, in the middle of which your nose, reassuringly, spouted red as usual. Swimming now was unadulterated pleasure – or maybe pleasure was just your new name for pain. You could feel yourself catching and overhauling the Australian, as if you were entering, then swimming through her body – at one moment you seemed to be in perfect congruence, with a double heartbeat and a headful of unfamiliar Antipodean thoughts. When you made the last turn the crowd roared again and you kicked on, but then you sensed the Canadian coming . . . for fifteen metres you were merged, one swimmer, but then, slowly, inexorably, you were swum through in your turn. It felt as if your own hips had shifted up around your ears. Afterwards, as the freestyle anchors bombed off down the pool, your rival's shining hands helped you out. You lay with your head in her lap as she held a towel to your gory nose, giving you a running commentary – with admirable objectivity – as Canada won and your team held off Australia for the silver. Her make-up fascinated you: why was a young girl impersonating a middle-aged woman impersonating a young girl, overlaying her natural freshness with its simulation? And how did all that powder and paint stay on through the race? You ran an index finger down her cheek. 'I know,' she shrugged, 'I hate it too but' – in a whisper – 'they pay me well to wear it.' For some reason, this lesser medal – or maybe this moment after your race was run – was just as precious to you as your gold.

At the post-games reception you found yourself running the gauntlet of a chain gang of mayors and aldermen: although they were all red-faced and fat they all felt cold and bony when they hugged you. They stared beyond your medals to your breasts. Then the throng parted and a small square woman a bit like Mum appeared: head down, eyes darting to and fro as if looking for a lost small dog, she grabbed your hand and muttered something inaudible from the side of her mouth. Only when you found yourself curtseying did you realize who it was: Godsaveourgracious, The Queen. You were mortified to feel liquid dripping down your face again, but then realized that it wasn't blood but tears. 'Patriotism is the last refuge of the scoundrel,' Dad had always said: nevertheless, you clung to her – were you imagining that gin reek on her breath? – and bawled.

Two days later, jet-lagged in Kentish Town, you were relieved to see no welcoming flags or bunting: the people on your street wouldn't have turned out for the second coming. Mum had changed the locks again so you had to knock and knock. The hall seemed to have shrunk and got darker: you kept bumping into Dad. Mum didn't look to have moved from the sofa since you'd left. You opened the velvet-lined cases and took out your medals. They shone like the sun and moon, illuminating the living room, mercilessly revealing the dust on the books and pictureframes, the stopped clock on the mantelpiece, the sienna-brown nicotine halo above Mum's

head, the spiders' webs, the line of white indentations like
bullet holes along the wall where the piano had stood. 'I
couldn't have done it without you,' you said and held out the
gold to Dad, but he wouldn't take it – he snarled, hissed and
recoiled like a vampire faced with garlic or the cross, the way
he did whenever Mrs Thatcher was mentioned. You placed
the medal on the armrest of his chair. Mum was weighing the
silver in the palm of her hand as if wondering how far she
could throw it.

You'd given Dad precise instructions of what, when and
how for the new video. Now, with a conjuror's gesture, he
inserted the cassette of your races. After a blare of music a
black-and-white picture of a pilotless aeroplane appeared: you
fast-forwarded, but there was only a succession of horrible
sweating faces, moving into and out of shadows. Dad had
erased your triumphs by – accidentally, he claimed – recording
an Orson Welles film on top. 'Shame,' he said, '*Confidential
Report* isn't much cop either. Except for Akim Tamiroff.'

Mum was saying how excited they'd got during the race,
but you weren't convinced. There was something second-hand
about the account, as if they'd only read or been told about

it. Had they forgotten or couldn't they be bothered even to walk across the room to turn it on? The gold medal had disappeared. You searched frantically until you found it, sunk deep into the recesses of the chair. In its wadding of fluff, withdrawn currency and peanuts, it glowed brighter than ever as if it had ingested all the light in the room. Dad snarled again – not in his Dracula routine this time, but unconsciously, the real thing. When you tried to close the cases both their clasps had broken, so you hung the medals round your neck for safety – their weight seemed to drag you down, as if the earth from which the metals had been torn was trying to draw them back. 'It's the Olympics that really count,' said Dad. 'The immutability of the Hellenic ideal.' Mum went to the toilet and didn't return: calling through the door, you got no response. You left Dad sitting in the darkness.

Later, the BBC presented you with the full tapes of heats and finals, tied with a huge pink ribbon bow, like the extravagant boxes of chocolates to which you were now treating yourself – if only provisionally, for you'd stick your fingers down your throat straight after gorging. The footage of your gold wasn't very exciting: just featureless heads bobbing up

and down a pool. You got the lanes confused and thought
for a moment that you hadn't won after all. It all looked so
smooth, so mechanical: your third length had been remarkably
fast – the quickest fifty you'd ever done – with the last, though
rather more rugged in style, not far behind. Nothing of what
had mattered showed up on screen: the real race had taken
place in your own head or inside your own body. And at the
ceremony your lips were in perfect sync with the anthem, and
your struggle not to laugh looked like a losing battle against
tears ... and when you met The Queen you seemed not to
be crying but laughing in her face.

For the first time, you rested through the winter break.
Having left school, you were now temping in the labyrinths
of the slab-Deco HQ of your former sponsors. It wasn't the
paradisical office of lovers of which you'd dreamed in the
park – you spent most of your days alone over the photocopier
– but at least you made a couple of friends in the typing pool
and, finally, had some money to splurge. You'd never thought
much about clothes, make-up and going out, but suddenly
you felt as if you'd been suffering years of deprivation. You
started to drink – Pernod and blackcurrant – and even smoke

– puffing on Balkan Sobranies: both tasted awful, but you'd read in a magazine that they were sophisticated. Swimming officials kept bursting in on you at work to check that you weren't doing any advertising or publicity: you had to send them all your bank statements and wage slips. They made you turn down all sorts of interesting offers, but did allow you to appear on 'Blue Peter' – where you disgraced yourself by laughing uncontrollably when one of the resident cats bit the presenter's finger to the bone – and on 'Sports Personality of the Year'. You'd come fifth: 'The tit-man vote,' said Coach.

When you did return to the water you seemed to have lost your buoyancy. It was as if your medals' solidity had spread through your body: strange heavinesses shifted around inside your legs – you thought you could hear them rattling like lead shot. A deep ache radiated from between your shoulder blades: sometimes you swooned or suffered palpitations and bad sweats. Although you hardly ate at all, you continued to put on weight: your nose even stopped bleeding. Medical science once more confessed itself baffled. As the first meet drew closer, however, you began to feel better: maybe, like most of the others, you'd begun to need the adrenaline of competition? But at the end of the race when you emerged in triumph – reckoning that you must have smashed not only your own record but Duncan Campbell's as well – it was to find yourself a bad fourth in a nothing field. Day by day, microsecond by microsecond, you were getting slower and slower. Coach spent less time with you and more with the younger girls. Raw-boned, as if their bodies had been folded out of cardboard, their white skins lined with raised blue veins, heavily moled and freckled – they were horrible, like aliens, but Coach and the water seemed to love them. They fell silent when you arrived and sniggered as you left: 'Psycho' had become once more a whispered insult. You were becoming an embarrassment, like a senile grandmother – just tolerated, while the family made the final arrangements with The Home. You felt as if you were a hundred years old: you were nineteen.

Coach didn't advise you to retire: he ordered you to. 'It's the shortest career there is,' he said, 'except for gymnasts and kamikaze pilots. You're unlucky: in a few years' time it'll all be professional and you'd be leaving as a millionaire.' You thought he was going to lock you in the room with a loaded revolver, but he just shook your hand again and then cupped your bottom in a valedictory squeeze. 'Still, you've got your medal. And you've got the looks. Go away and cash in. You've earned it.'

'Is the future still a straight line?' you asked him, but he only looked blank – apparently he didn't remember his own slogans.

You turned up for that evening's training as usual, but ignored the group work, drifting out into the furthest lane where you drove yourself relentlessly up and down the pool. But there was no pleasure or pain in it any more: the silver glow didn't appear. Never again would you swim out of or back into your body – or anyone else's. No matter how hard you tried, all you could do was coast. The water was bidding you a kind but impersonal farewell, like the vicar had after Gran's funeral. After an hour, you swam to the side and climbed out, as slowly as if you'd been ascending a scaffold. Coach made all the other girls applaud, but you walked to the changing-room without a backward glance. You felt nothing: no regret or relief, no nostalgia or anticipation. That afternoon you'd worked out that in competition and practice you'd swum something like 12,000 miles, almost half the circumference of the world. According to Dad's Atlas, that would have put you right in the centre of the Pacific Ocean, with Midway Island approximately the nearest shore. Forward or back, you were a long way from home.

11

ON YOUR FIRST HOLIDAY FOR ten years you lay among the tandooried bodies like a leper, glaring at the distant white line of sea as if it were an old boyfriend who'd chucked you: but although you kept cutting it dead it never noticed. You couldn't take the Costa Brava sun – even under Factor ×15 it felt like boiling water pouring on to your skin – so you left your friends and retreated to the hotel. For the rest of the week you read the first fifty pages of *Papillon* – you'd bought it for the cover, but it was merely about escaping convicts – and went to bed with five different men. Or perhaps it had been one man in five disguises: they all said and did the same things, in roughly the same order. And they all looked the same when their clothes came off: grey, hairy and slab-like, their skin stretched or slackened in surprising places, as if every bone beneath had been broken and then poorly reset. Two of them were – they said – celebrities like yourself: a Capital Radio DJ and a recently-sacked manager of Manchester City. They were at least twice your age: you'd reckoned that you could trust them to know how to do it, but Coach – as far as you could remember – seemed to have been all too representative. Sex was turning out to be a disappointment: you'd hoped it would feel like the final lap of your gold medal swim – including the cheering.

Perhaps it was your own fault: maybe you were frigid or somehow physically impaired? Perhaps you should go with the boys, like your friends did? But they all just gaped at you like they did at the limos in the car park, like beggars who knew that they'd always be out in the cold. Finally, on your last night, you dragged a drunken but tolerable teenager off the disco floor and up to your room. You manoeuvred him carefully into position, but he came as he was rolling on the condom. It was true what they said about youth's greater regenerative powers though – he did the same thing three times in the next ten minutes before losing consciousness. You dragged him into the corridor and left him. When you went to catch your flight the following morning he was still lying there, with a beatific smile, asleep.

Coach had given you the name of a good manager. You tracked him down by following the sour-milk smell to a cupboard-sized office at the top of a stairwell in St Martin's Lane. At first you thought you were the victim of a practical joke: he looked exactly like Coach, except that there seemed to be a third, pineal eye peeping through the thick convergence of his brows. 'I can make you the second Esther Williams,' he said. You tried to look pleased, although you'd never heard of the first. He handed you a cheque and three laminated sheets of addresses and instructions. Clothes: reds, silvers and blacks . . . short and low, tight but classy. Heels: always high. Rings and jewellery: never anything but gold. There was a deck of membership cards and vouchers: Fitness Fantasy, Cute Cuticles, Sol's Sauna – 20% discount on the eighteen-tube all-over Max-Tan . . . 50% off leg-waxing and depilation. 'Your hair has to be shorter,' he said, 'but still long enough for' – he rolled his eyes – 'bunches . . . Oh, and you need to be blonde, of course.' But you were blonde. 'That's yellow, not blonde' – he handed you another card – 'Tell them the usual with . . . ash highlights.'

'Was Esther Williams a blonde?' you asked.

He thought about it: 'I can't remember . . . but I suppose she must have been.'

London didn't feel like your home: you couldn't imagine it feeling like home to anybody. It was as if everyone on the streets was engaged in a strenuous competition, to which you were an audience of one – watching them as they had until recently been watching you. But all their strivings remained incomprehensible to you: there wasn't a start or a finish and there didn't seem to be any rules. At Russell Square station one morning you realized that seven other women, line abreast, were waiting with you for the lift. Some had their eyes shut, the one next to you appeared to be mouthing a silent prayer – all had tension or fear in their faces . . . when the steel doors at last folded back you had to stop yourself from spear-diving straight in: nothing was that simple any more. Compared with everyone else your movements and reactions seemed to be painfully slow: since your retirement,

your knees and hips had stiffened up and years of chlorine
infections and water impact had left you partially deaf. As if
sensing easy pickings, gropers zeroed in on you, scientologists
offered you free personality tests, lunatics gibbered at you.
One day, wherever you went, the same mad head kept popping
out of the scrum to ask, 'Did you know that the sun is only
sixteen miles away from earth?' You finally replied that it
looked a lot closer to you. After you'd been given the usual
with ash highlights – by an ex-Sassoon cutter who said the
hairdressing establishment was persecuting him 'because I'm
like Galileo and they can't face the truth' – you found yourself
stranded for ten minutes in the middle of Victoria Street. It
wasn't the noise and rush that had frozen you, but the illusion
that the traffic island was surrounded by fast-running water
and that you'd forgotten how to swim. It was as if you'd just
come out of jail – having done your time, done your time –
and were having to relearn everything.

After the full makeover you looked older, harder and more
worldly-wise, although you didn't feel to have learnt anything.
Dad pretended not to notice any difference, but Mum went
wild. It was the first time you'd ever seen her laugh properly

– at best she'd only sounded like someone reading HA-HA off an optician's chart – but as she turned purple and threw her arms about it was more disturbing than anything else – especially as she showed no sign of stopping. 'What is it you'll be doing, exactly?' Dad asked.

Your manager had been vague: 'A bit of everything . . . acting . . . modelling . . . advertising . . . promo-ing . . .'

Dad looked up sharply: 'There's no such word.' So you leafed through the *OED*, then triumphantly flicked it with one of your new two-inch scarlet nails: 'PROMO (Adjective): Promotional (sb. publishing, advertising)'.

Dad sniffed: 'An adjective, though, not a verb. So although it can be said to exist, nobody actually does it.' You resisted the temptation to turn to the entry for WELKIN. 'Still,' he conceded, 'whatever it is, I suppose it's better than working in some concentration camp of the soul.' From behind the toilet door you could hear Mum spluttering, as she tried unsuccessfully to drink and laugh at the same time.

At six the next morning you were in a red velvet ball gown, posing for the external shots of your publicity portfolio on the bridge over the lake in St James's Park. It was deserted except for a couple of sleeping tramps who had to be woken and bribed to move out of the frame. At the shutter's first click, the rising sun hit and held you in its spotlight. Then it was back to the studio, where – for the first of countless times – you declined to go topless. 'It's just for the lighting,' said the cameraman mysteriously, 'just so you'll know.'

At lunch, the adjoining tables in the restaurant were filled with faces you recognized, although you could put a name to almost none. As you were inserted for photographs into each group in turn they froze in a toothy tableau like the cardboard cutouts in the arcades on Worthing seafront. One thing annoyed you: your manager kept introducing you as 'the Olympic Gold Medallist'. 'I have to do it,' he said. 'It's the only thing they'll have heard of. If there's ever a problem just tell them it was the Commonwealth Olympics.'

Then you were off to your first assignment, to the outskirts of Milton Keynes, to open a new Homes and Garden DIY superstore. In the back of your manager's sea-green Merc you changed into your swimsuit: you noticed that his eyes didn't stray to the driving-mirror. On arrival they gave you a gold-painted hard hat that kept slipping down over your eyes. Your half-exposed bottom was being constantly pinched, but when you wheeled round there was never anyone close enough to have done it, no one looking guilty or smug. Maybe the place was haunted? The empty, seemingly infinite aisles did have a spooky feel: much of the stock looked like torture equipment – and how could there be sixty-two different shades of white paint? You'd always thought that white was white. Still, you waggled the drills and spikes enthusiastically, rammed a garden fork into the concrete floor and buckled its prongs, bent over saucily with a watering can and contrived to look impressed by the world's longest hosepipe. Your costume felt as though it was shrinking, biting deep into your goose-pimpled shoulder blades and perineum, and your nipples, aching, seemed to have swollen to thumb-size, but you just kept giggling. When you came to cut the tape across the entrance the shears they'd given you proved too blunt – so were the next pair and the next. A salesman brandished a Swiss Army knife but, merely ran its corkscrew into his palm, so that, finally, you had to rip it open with your hands, losing three nail-enhancements in the process. Your laughter and the cheers of the crowd set great echoes rolling round the high-vaulted ceiling. And you were doubly delighted, for your nose had once again begun to bleed. Promo-ing! Even if it wasn't quite the Commonwealth Games, at least there was some excitement left in the world!

Then you were driving back to town for your evening LBC interview, both of you still laughing, with a clear road ahead. You kept calling him Coach and then apologizing, but he said he preferred it to his name – 'less syllables' – and wanted to keep it. Suddenly other cars converged like clouds, enveloping and immobilizing you. The radio was dead and the mobile phone – the first you'd ever seen – only crackled with static and feedback. It was an hour before police loudspeakers informed you that the IRA had placed a bomb under the motorway pillars above Brent Cross. You were gridlocked for three more hours, missing your interview: you were willing to jog it, but New Coach wouldn't let you, even though you offered to carry him piggyback. While you grizzled, he beat the wheel with frustration: 'Irish bastards! What did we ever do to them?' For the whole time, the people in the lanes next to you – a family of four whose side windows were largely obscured by Arsenal stickers, and a rep type with his suit and spare white shirt hanging in the back – never once glanced across, just sat staring straight ahead.

That night, as recompense or reward, Coach took you to a famous jazz club in Soho. It was as dark and obstacle-strewn as Mum and Dad's hallway, furnace-hot and full of choking caporal smoke – the noisy fan only made it worse, like a sirocco. There was a tremendous bedlam of voices from no apparent source, but the party of Scandinavian youths at the next table never spoke at all, just wrote things on a succession of postcards and passed them to one another. Coach asked the waitress for his usual, which turned out to be an enormous chip and ketchup sandwich and a litre of rough Aussie Red. And you'd thought it was going to be sophisticated . . . you stuck to Perrier. The musicians finally appeared: a dozen very thin black men in painted masks and tie-dyed robes who proceeded to play loud, fast and completely unrelated things, then periodically threw down their instruments to conga round the room, chanting about how they'd just flown in from the sun. You felt like telling them that you knew that it was a shorter journey than the one from Milton Keynes. Coach was tapping his foot and nodding appreciatively, though he did confide that he was really more of a Sarah Vaughan–Slim Gaillard man. As you left, the Scandinavians were beginning, silently, to fight. You didn't dare go to the Ladies' because some of the band were sitting on the stairs.

Shaftesbury Avenue – even at 2.30 a.m., midweek – was crowded, not just with clubbers but with seemingly all types and conditions of people, flowing towards Trafalgar Square, as if for some mass meeting. It was sinister, like some science-fiction film: you were sure you'd seen the family from the motorway among them. Linking arms, you forced your way across to St Martin's Lane. There, in the office, you bent over the desk – minimizing the pressure on your bursting bladder – while Coach took you from behind. It was as brief and impersonal as an inoculation and you knew that it was the first and last time – to get it out of the way, to make sure that nothing would undermine your business relationship. You didn't feel abused: there was a strange, impressive gravity about it. You understood that it was – after the handshake and the signature – the third seal.

'A full date-book is a happy pro,' New Coach liked to say. Every day there were new people, new things, new places, so you knew that you were happy. And – magazines, television, posters – you were everywhere. You perched in the jaws of a mechanical digger ... you riding a mountain bike down a glass-sheeted swimming pool ... you kneeling by an oven, in floral gloves, inserting or extracting tasty flans – the bump of your left knee seemed to delineate the face of an ancient Chinaman, exciting millenarianists ... you in a little black dress with a row of nicotine patches up your arm like a family of leeches – after this session you started to smoke again, inhaling this time. Your ears, your bum, your legs – but never your feet: 'Too big and boaty' they said ... Your shoulders, your hands, your breasts – always well-concealed but some-how always the focal point, looking larger and more conical than they really were ... And, always, your mouth – the lips and now-capped teeth smiling the new smile they'd been taught.

The former, extirpated model had photographed, they said, as a red triangle sliding off your chin. 'Where on earth did you get a smile like that?' asked the isometric girl. 'It was a present,' you replied: you'd always assumed that your smile, like your soul, was just 'there'. Learning all your new expressions hadn't been easy: your face ached – yet more nerves and muscles you didn't know you had announced themselves through pain. The champings and silent screams hurt worse than the old circuits: sitting before the mirror you realized that you were producing a low continuous humming noise like a water purification system. 'Looking natural is bloody hard work,' said Coach – he shared Coach One's fondness for aphorism and paradox. You were frightened that the smile would set into a permanent rictus: once, woken by a wrong number, you knew by the tightness in your jaw and eye sockets that it had possessed you in the night.

There were some disappointments. The talk of your own named line of sports and casual wear came to nothing: swimming didn't require enough equipment or accessories and what there was scored low on style. And when they tried you out for the waterproof cosmetic range – you hoped that the Canadian girl hadn't been dropped – it ran all over your face, nearly blinding you, leaving white clumps on your skin like in the bad old Cheesy years. But that very afternoon – for a fee you could hardly believe – you landed your first mail-order catalogue. Doing it was hell, though: a full six weeks of twelve-hour days, with the marketing men like fanatical priests, too humourless and driven even to fumble you, and the clothes you modelled so nasty – even the odd thing that looked OK then felt especially horrible. You hoped that your expressions might convey subliminal warnings – this ridges up at the back, that crackles with static electricity, this is falling apart after two minutes, these have seam-stitches like rivets – but your new, natural smile just airbrushed all nuances away.

Your quickie as-told-to autobiography appeared: you merely skimmed its 135 pages. As you'd suspected, it bore no relation to your own life: the journalist had turned off the tape whenever you'd tried to talk about the important things. Dad had been recast as an inspirational coach with unusual training methods, Mum as an inexhaustible fount of sage advice and can-do motivation . . . and what fun it had been in the squad! The pranks, the camaraderie, the nicknames! . . . Dutifully, you went on daytime TV to plug it: the questions they asked you were at once too general and too trivial – proudest, worst, funniest, most embarrassing moments? – and you numbly recited your prepared responses – meeting The Queen, losing to drug cheats, the day that your costume had evaporated mid-race. You felt as if it had all happened to someone else. Coach tried to get you on 'This Is Your Life' but failed: you were relieved because, at twenty-one, surely it had hardly started. Dad kept going on about it: 'Eamonn's red book might have a gold medal on the cover, but inside there'd be nothing but blank pages.' You just smiled your smile because he didn't even know that Eamonn Andrews – or Seamus Android as he called him, in an execrable Irish accent – was no longer doing the programme, being many years dead.

Three months later, when you'd almost forgotten about them, a crate of catalogues were dumped at your door, much to Dad's delight. 'Four hundred and twenty-eight pages,' he said, 'and not a single beautiful thing on any of them!' He was wrong, though: there was just one. Your first appearance was on page fourteen, beaming ecstatically in the sort of boned, elastoplast-pink underwear Mum used to favour, while over on page fifteen – in hideous strobing candy-striped jockeys and a vest of what appeared to be plaited vermicelli – was a man. He reminded you of Tom, Nik Kershaw and the boy in the park, although he was nothing like any of them. Even from the photograph you knew that he must be tall: his gawky limbs seemed to have been folded to fit into the frame and to be now pushing rebelliously against its edges. There was a curious stippling like long-healed acne scars in the declivities of his shoulders and neck. His eyelashes were impossibly long and seemed to issue from his lower lids. You felt as if every significant question in the world was being posed and then answered in the shadows under his cheekbones. Alone among the dozen or so models, he couldn't or wouldn't smile. You were facing each other: across the pages your gazes met. With Dad's magnifying glass you were sure that you could see your embarrassingly-garbed figures reflected in each other's eyes. You imagined an unbroken line of laser-thin light burning through the mass of corseted flesh between you. 'I think he's off one of the Aussie soaps,' said Coach, 'in episodes that haven't been shown here yet. Gay, I hear.' So you were in different hemispheres, but it didn't matter: you could feel his presence, as if he were only two inches of glossy paper away.

You kept the catalogue at your bedside like a bible. Every night you read it as a narrative – of two human lives played out in the interstices of cheap merchandise, a doomed love story like Yuri and Lara in your second favourite video, *Doctor Zhivago*. Across the subsequent pages you tirelessly tracked each other – sometimes just missing, sometimes far apart. You were on the piste in what looked and felt like an inflatable straitjacket, but he was on a yacht, squinting under a dreadful shiny-peaked cap . . . you swam towards him, but now he was playing tennis, motionless as the ball flashed by, lost in dreams of you . . . in boots that pinched you climbed a rocky hill, but he was mooching in an autumnal forest, kicking up the dead leaves. You both met others and tried to love them: you were dogged by a sleek, shark-headed criminal-type, while he was often attended by a distaff second self, a ponytailed jailbait kid sister. Unsatisfied, you both sought consolation in shopping: you collected clocks and watches, all of which seemed to have stopped at noon or midnight, while he assembled the perfect stereo system. One night, staring at his picture on page 383 – he was apprehensively peeping into an orange plastic picnic hamper as if it was Pandora's Box – you discovered that if you held it up to the light, from overleaf, your smiling mouth appeared in the centre of his forehead. These were your final appearances: there was to be no happy ending. Children's Toys and Games made up the last section: the catalogue ended in mechanical apocalypse and a riot of garishly-coloured animals and dolls.

At about this time cardboard cutouts of yourself – in leotard, dirndl and glasses – began to appear in the windows of a chain of opticians. That these figures were slightly larger than life-size you took as an implicit criticism, but even more disturbing was the fact that you couldn't remember ever having posed for the shot. Your name was there, in tiny red letters under your bare toes: how could you have forgotten those frames – enormous, butterfly-winged Edna Everage style? Your vision might have been twenty-twenty, but your memory seemed to be going. You checked back through your date-book, but it was just a meaningless sequence of names, places and times which triggered no memories or associations at all. This coincided with the launch of your biggest-ever poster campaign: GOOD GIRLS DRINK MILK. You were sitting, looking just-tumbled, in a hayloft – you did remember that session because the dust had brought your allergies on – downing a calcium-rich pinta – of coloured water, as the taste and even the smell of milk had always nauseated you. It seemed strange that no one recognized you in the street: the few who did approach had usually mistaken you for a TV weather forecaster. You would have needed to have been fifty feet tall for them to have made the connection. People you met knew that you were something, but weren't sure what: if you told them that you were the swimmer, they just looked blank, as if it might have been a euphemism or a joke they didn't get.

Even if they didn't know you, the crowds still cheered when you arrived for charity premières at the Leicester Square Odeon or the Café Royale, on the arm of your putative boy-friend, a gay former skating champion and fellow-client, now vainly trying to bankroll his own ice show. Coach was cooking up a media romance: king of the surface meets queen of the deep, fire melts ice and so forth – he projected a white marriage, soon-to-be shattered – after the cosy domestic television and magazine features – by sensational divorce proceedings, with a Page Three Girl – another client, with an upcoming exercise video nicely tying-in – as third party. Unfortunately, the skater got outed, then got AIDS.

New Coach wasn't as much fun as Old Coach. Although he'd never attempted to touch you again, he kept trying to talk you into doing nude shots. 'It's glamour modelling. Don't you want to be glamorous?' He drew everyone into the conspiracy: one lunch time you saw the skater's boyfriend lacing your Indian tonics with vodka, after which the Page Three Girl just happened along and tried to sweep you off to her afternoon session: 'I'm not ashamed of my body. That's why I like to celebrate it.' They were all so serious about it, as if getting your bra off was a point of principle for them. It made no sense: you wouldn't have got the milk posters or the catalogues if you'd ever gone topless – they'd vetted you for 'wholesomeness' beforehand. 'The catalogues won't be there forever,' said Coach, 'but your tits will.' You had a mental picture of a post-apocalypse world empty of everything except your eternal breasts . . . but even then you'd ensure that they'd remain under wraps: it had become a point of principle for you too.

Another strange thing about Coach was his insistence on your being photographed again and again in St James's Park. Some nights he'd drive you there himself and snap away in the darkness with his own 35 mm. Apparently he did this with all his clients: you puzzled over what its significance could be.

Was his first memory of feeding the ducks there with Mummy? Or had he met or parted from the love of his life on that narrow bridge? Was he hoping that one day some trace of a lost something might show up on the developed film? When you finally gathered the courage to ask, he just replied, non-committally: 'Quiet. Good sightlines. I just think it's a nice location.'

The best thing about your new life was your car. Driving had come as easily to you as swimming. After only twenty minutes behind the wheel, your jolly, patronizing instructor had fallen silent with a hurt and angry look – like Mum's at Worthing – on his face. When you reverse-parked flawlessly in a tiny space you thought that he was going to burst into tears. He refused to teach you again, accusing you of winding him up: borrowing Coach's Merc you passed your test regardless. To be once again fantastic at something – 'a natural' – meant so much to you: you felt as if you'd been stumbling aimlessly about, only to slip suddenly and effortlessly into a preordained place. You trusted that your life would be a succession of such transformations: that you would prove to be a natural at many other things – at love, marriage, motherhood, happiness. And you knew that a man was coming – your man, your mate, your other half – in whose arms you'd feel the same wholeness and sense of return as in the water or in the driver's seat. If the catalogue model wasn't the one, then you knew he'd been a prophet, a signal that your wait would soon be over. Every day suddenly made sense as a countdown from an unknown number.

Other people's driving seemed to be about self-assertion and aggression – Coach couldn't go a hundred yards without cutting up someone with more hair or a better motor – but to you it brought serenity. London no longer bothered you: from behind the wheel it had become a very different place. Your car was like a bathyscape in which you descended to the ocean floor to observe the strange life forms flickering to and fro. You felt that, if danger threatened, you could always escape back to the surface. You called your car The Fish, after the mysterious acronym on its papers – which turned out to mean Full Insurance and Service History. You talked with it all the time – just brisk, factual observations or route suggestions, nothing soppy . . . neither of you needed to say how you felt. It had given you a new confidence: you felt as if part of it had entered you, like in your childhood exchange with the water. You were stronger, moving faster: sometimes you'd be surprised by the sight of your large feet padding away below, for you half-expected to be running on tyres. You started wearing more and brighter reds – although Coach said it looked corny – to match The Fish's colour. What you liked most was – before you even turned the ignition key – just to sit in it and then put on your safety-belt. When you heard the clunk-click and felt your heart beating against the webbing's gentle embrace you knew that everything was going to be all right.

You bought your own flat: an attic in Chelsea. Although it was north-facing, the sun's rays obligingly glanced off the windows opposite to flood your tiny front room with light. When you told Mum that you were moving out, she called you a whore and punched you, closed-fist, in the face: her wedding-ring's garnets split your lip. At least it was preferable to that terrible laughter. 'Try not to blame her,' said Dad, as he helped you to pack. 'It's just that she worries about you . . . and we've rather come to rely on the rent.' All your stuff easily fitted into The Fish: apart from your clothes and make-up there were only a few videos, your cuttings-books, the medals in their cases. It didn't look like very much. Suddenly, for the first time in twelve years, you thought of Buddenbrooks, your discarded teddy bear, remembering his square ears, chewed furless, and the extruded left eye dangling on its wire. You insisted on searching the attic for him, but there were only empty gin bottles, locked suitcases and dust. When you came down, cobwebbed, tearful, still bleeding, Dad silently handed you Volume One of the *Collected Works of Thomas Mann*. Driving back towards the river you and The Fish somehow lost yourselves among the familiar streets, turning desperately left–left–left until you finally hit the Edgware Road. The way was lined with those images of you gulping down the fake milk, of your smile below the spectacles of clear glass. They began to unnerve you: it was as if wherever you went you were already there, waiting – numberless fractured and separated other selves were looming up enormous and ghostly in your headlights, to threaten, mock or warn.

Coach – everyone called him that now, he even had it on his business cards – kept on trying to break you into television. You had lots of walk-ons in comedies or game shows, waving to the viewers as if you or they were embarking on a long voyage. And you kept smiling your smile, smiling your smile. On 'A Question of Sport', you didn't get a single answer correct – not even the ones on swimming, failing to recognize a clip of your old Canadian rival. 'I never knew much about it,' you said, 'I just used to do it' – at which everyone threw themselves about in simulated mirth. Later, in the Green Room, another panellist, the ex-footballer, grinned at you: 'I know you knew 'em all really. It's a sort of Esther Williams meets Goldie Hawn act, isn't it? My act is being a drunk' – he drained his glass and, winking a purple-lidded eye, reached for another – 'convincing, isn't it?'

You weren't a natural for television. When speaking to camera you seemed to be possessed by a demon that could only say er and um, and your eyes would bulge – as if in a horror film – and then slowly begin to cross. You looked alternately wired with tension and bonelessly relaxed and, as you'd dreaded, your smile had gone out of control – it came and went as it pleased, seeming to appreciate disaster and tragedy while taking a dim view of jokes and fun. You did roving reports for Breakfast TV: commentating on a charity

tug-of-war on Brighton Beach you tangled up the microphone
cable with the rope and brought the whole thing to a crashing,
cursing, exploding halt. Back in the studio the anchor duo
watched stony-faced: they knew it wasn't calculated ditsiness,
they knew you were miserable and terrified. 'Better get back
in the water, love,' one of them said, 'because you're drowning
out there.' They shifted you to the kiddies' segment: grotesque
screaming puppets groped you above the table while their
operators groped you below. When you finally stamped on
them the puppets groaned. Your last, doomed venture was to
introduce – in kohl, black lipstick, fingerless gloves and what
looked like a trawling net – a pilot heavy metal showcase. It
went out at three a.m. on Tyne-Tees and was never shown
again, but sacks of weird mail ensued – anything franked
Newcastle went straight into your bin, unopened.

The advertising and promotional work began to fall off.
Consumer surveys after the second series of milk ads showed
that your recognition factor had declined. 'The punters still
like you,' said Coach, 'they just don't know who you are or
what you did.' When you asked him why the companies
couldn't just put your name on the posters, he shook with

mirthless laughter. 'You sell the product,' he finally coughed out, 'the product doesn't sell you.'

At least the managers and doormen of the clubs and discos up West knew who you were all right. Your signed photographs were hung in the foyers and over the bars – usually the one taken on the bridge that first morning, of you jumping into the air, arms flung open wide, legs tucked up behind, head thrown back, with your old crooked smile just distinguishable in the movement blur. Everyone said that it radiated youth, joy and freshness, but you thought of it to yourself as the Floating Amputee. Every night you went out, walking past the queues and straight inside – free, on the nod. And, throughout the long, delirious hours that followed, whenever you felt hungry or thirsty, hands would magically appear with trays of Twiglets and glasses of spritzer.

Although you weren't a natural at dancing, you loved it as much as driving. It made all the aches and pains disappear, released all the energy unused in being photographed and looked at: galvanic, uncoordinated, you frugged wildly even through the smoochy numbers. A pro once tried unsuccessfully to put you right: arms in, head steady on the neck, unclench the fists, never lift the feet – just shuffle or slide, don't bend the knees, keep the mouth shut, try not to blink – the only things that could move, apparently, were your hips. You continued to dance as if wrestling with an invisible adversary, much stronger, but allowing you for a while to hold your own. Sometimes a huge hand seemed to pluck you up and hang you on an unseen peg: the lights were dimmed and flickered so no one could observe such levitations. As it got hotter and the off-beat kept jerking you into and out of your body, the cigarette smoke turned from blue to grey, stopped drifting and formed a solid wall like those last-lap fogs. Your requests took up half the night: 'Feel', of course – 'Float On' by The Floaters – and, always, your beloved Diana Ross. Not the early Motown stuff that Dad liked, wrecked by rooting baritone saxes, but 'Inside Out', 'Chain Reaction' and – most important of all, a signal that you knew your man would recognize – 'I'm Still Waiting'.

At the end of the song, you would open your eyes only to discover that the awaited one still hadn't arrived, although someone else usually had. Just as you'd had to compete in order to be in the water, so the attentions of men were the toll that was exacted for dancing. Why did so many go for Shakespeare – Romeo under the balcony or Sonnet 18 – as their opening chat-up line? They'd weave and flinch from your flailing arms: 'Dancing with you is like going twelve with Alan Minter.' 'Thanks,' you replied. After the last number you'd usually kiss your partner passionately, excuse yourself to The Powder Room and walk straight out of the exit. If you ever met again you'd cut him: if he persisted, you'd put your face in your hands and let your shoulders shake – tears always got rid of them.

Sometimes, though, you went home with them: always your place, never theirs. If you'd drunk enough you could half-convince yourself that this might be, if not the long-awaited one, then at least a bearer of tidings – but usually you were reassuring yourself that you weren't missing out on anything and that unlike your one-night partners – whose subsequent desperate phone messages and cards you always ignored – your loneliness was a matter of choice. Being in control was fun: asking them to pick a record and then playing something else, instigating and breaking off every embrace, knocking the hands away and then putting them back in the same place.

You'd teach them how to butterfly-kiss: the eyelashes fanning over your cheeks and brow were like soft brushes, sweeping you clean – you could have laid like that forever, but they all started whining that blinking became agonizing after a couple of minutes.

You'd start on the sofa and then – if you were feeling particularly romantic – move on to but never into the bed. The thought of someone else's body sliding between your sheets made you feel sick: you wished that the prophylactics that they donned with such reluctance could be stretched to cover their entire bodies. Once the clothes were off even the most promising just fell apart: what little rigidity they had went into their thrusting bone or jabbing tongue, while the rest of their gelid flesh eddied and sloshed around you. None could even manage to suck your nipples hard enough, and their body hair didn't abrade but clung and adhered as if trying to effect a more insidious interchange. Where was the solidity you craved, the strong man against whose granite but kindly chest you could dash yourself into unconsciousness? Sometimes you amused yourself by expanding and contracting your ribcage to trampoline your grunting partners up and down: you felt as if you could have scissored them in two at the waist with your swimmer's legs or, by raising one knee, bifurcated them – you imagined the separated halves worming off in opposite directions.

They never made you come, although sometimes you'd put on an insultingly bad pretence. You kept your eyes shut throughout, trying to recall the features of the boys in the catalogue and the park. When it was all over, you were always surprised to find your partner still there, as if a dream had run on beyond awakening or a dinner you'd just eaten was still sitting on your plate. 'I need my beauty sleep,' you'd say – although even with the pills you hardly slept at all – and push him out. First Coach remained the only man you'd ever spent a night with. As soon as the door closed you'd strip the candlewick cover from the bed and plunge it into the bath, half-filled with cold water, ready. Then, silently, you'd bring yourself off with your fingers, again and again, until you ached.

Your assignments were fewer now, and different. You spent more time with cars – not nice like Fish, but crude, expensive, swollen-looking ones. In tiny skirts and scalloped tops you crawled over their bonnets, sat on their roofs and – always on the passenger side – clambered in and out. You adorned motorcycles: propping against one dream-machine, custom-made for square-arsed killer robots, the photographer requested that you 'spread your legs wider and think wet'. Your effort to comply just knocked the bike over. You made a record: a version of 'Float On'. But you didn't sound like Diana Ross – your voice was a karaokefied helium squeak over hideous bubbling, fruity sound-effects like someone farting in a bath. You didn't want the accompanying video to be shot in the water, but to have a flying theme instead. 'You're Esther Williams, not Amelia Earhart,' Coach said. So you found yourself once again in Crystal Palace pool at dawn – but this time in the company of twelve panicking, floundering nose-clipped hunks. You were wearing a mermaid tail that really smelt, disturbingly, of fish, and a seaweedy green wig, its trailing ends glued on to your breasts. Although you still thought of yourself as being a swimmer, you now realized that this no longer had anything to do with the water – you got cramp and nearly went down with the hunks, explaining that you were used to moving about not standing in it.

At least you finally saw Esther Williams: the video director showed you a clip from *Dangerous When Wet*. She looked a bit like poor Karen – mousy-haired, flabby-thighed – and was dancing underwater with Tom The Cat and Jerry Mouse, being menaced by a cartoon squid in a beret, with a seductive French accent. It cheered you up: after all, things could be worse – but then Coach got you into panto in Romford, as Cinder's Fairy Godmother, sharing the bill with your old friends, the TV puppets. By the end of the winter their operators were black and blue, traumatized – and you'd flown at last, nightly, on a wire that kept nearly garrotting you while you sang 'Float On', which had, on release, sunk like a stone.

The gaps in your date-book increased: you filled them with gym sessions – there was nowhere to dance in London during the day. At 'Fitness Fantasy' you pushed, pumped iron, pressed, bench-thrusted, pulled. There was no fantasy about it – you hunted fitness down implacably, as if it was a fugitive from your justice. 'Stupidity! Stolidity! Senselessness!' – as you sweated, in violent contention with the machines, Dad's alternative Three Ss kept running through your head, to the tune of 'God Save The Queen'. It was a different feeling from your swimming days: instead of gaining suppleness it was as if you were becoming a solid form like a sculpture. People asked why you were back in training: you didn't like to tell them what you thought – that you were preparing yourself to be loved. Your man still hadn't appeared, but now in the gym you felt that you were somehow halving the waiting time, counting up as well as down, driving yourself towards him.

'Tight and firm's all well and good,' Coach worried, 'but you're getting like a bagful of chisels. A face that says maybe and a body that says yes is what we want – not a face that says yes and a body that says no way, José.' You began running in the evenings and early mornings, enjoying it now as much as once you'd hated it. Your feet pummeled the pavement like jackhammers, with some internal tachometer registering every fifty metres. Although you carried a whistle and a Mace spray, men didn't bother you: perhaps by the time they were reacting you'd gone. Along the Embankment you'd pass a billboard of the newest milk poster. A youth-TV presenter – another blonde with ash highlights – was your successor: she was sticking out her celebrated foot-long tongue to lick at the slogan, 'Bad Girls Drink Milk'. Perhaps it had taken her years of pain and self-denial to achieve this, perhaps she had a sideboard piled with cups and medals from tongue-stretching championships, but you felt that you were also in training to be able to rip the thing from the wall and send that wagging crimson spike spinning into the stratosphere.

Your last endorsement – the muesli – wasn't renewed: you threw away the remaining complimentary cartons and never ate breakfast again. Now only the glamour photographers and men in Newcastle wanted you: Coach didn't even take you to St James's Park any more. You had even more time for the gym: you spent and spent on clothes – all red; you got blonder and blonder, through platinum towards albino. You traded in The Fish for Fish Two, a perfect colour-match for your new lipstick, Paloma Picasso's Mon Rouge, and Y reg with a personalized number plate: 605WIM. You stuck cheeky slogans in the back and side windows: BABE ON BOARD, HONK IF YOU WANT IT, SWIMMERS DO IT IN THE WATER – although you were doing it less and less and didn't want it at all.

'You're fronting it,' said Coach, 'but at least you're still making an effort.' He was still fighting his war of attrition against your clothes, endlessly nagging about bras and knickers, as if trying to argue them away, fibre by fibre. He finally did for you with the thong. On a calendar-shoot for the oil company, your old sponsors, he suddenly shook his fist in your face, then smilingly opened it to reveal the tiny garment, like a burst red balloon, lying in the palm of his hand. 'It won't be in the magazines: it's only for trade . . . Just a bit of fun . . . And artistic . . . and I've got you the best month – May.' They had you kneeling on the beach with the company's logo picked out in sand – or, rather, glitter – on your bottom cheeks: 'You'll be less than quarter-profile: no one will know it's you' . . . And there, at last, you surrendered – 'It's only for a back shot' – and took off your top, hoping that Mr Right would understand and forgive.

These days virtually every man you met tried it on with you, even the ugly and the poor: how could they think you were available when everything about you signalled that you were out of their league? Even schoolboys ogled you, while old men dropped their gaze and muttered curses. Your parents' next-door neighbour, who'd never said more than good morning, suddenly lunged at you, bugging his eyes and making a noise like a soda siphon. When you complained, Dad just said, 'Why get yourself up like that if you don't want attention?' while Mum went into her laughing routine. It was two years since you'd left, and she still wasn't talking to you, but there were some positive signs. She wasn't returning your cheques and would now usually slam a cup of tea in front of you, although it was either unsugared or a sweet sludge that was impossible to stir – you drank it down regardless. Dad rabbited on about things you neither knew nor cared about: it was as if he just turned on a loudspeaker to broadcast his ceaseless interior monologue. They now took it in turns to make long visits to the bathroom: you found Mum's gin in its usual place and Dad's – a different brand – wrapped in a vest at the bottom of the laundry basket. They couldn't share anything: not even their secret drinking.

Even in the clubs you'd begun to lose control: the men gathered like sharks scenting blood in the water. Some walked up and grabbed your tits without preamble, others bowed and made as if to kiss your hand but then forced it down their trousers. One that you did allow back insisted on taking things at his own pace, looking at his watch the while, and left with a snigger before you ordered him out: only afterwards did it occur to you that it might have been rape. Although you subsequently always went home alone, you soon realized that you had acquired the worst reputation of all – as yet another groper kindly informed you after you'd had to slap him, you were well known for being 'a frigid slag'. You left, setting Fish Two to drive purposelessly into the featureless suburbs, turning left-right-left-right, as if trying to shake off a pursuer, until the first light appeared in the sky and – right-left-right-left – you returned.

The BBC had hired you as an expert summarizer for the swimming events in the Commonwealth Games. It was now four years since your gold – it seemed as if it had been only yesterday, but also as if it had never happened at all. You'd hoped for a free holiday in Australia, but it was to be merely a week of early mornings in an airless studio in Shepherd's Bush. Coach wanted you to wear your shortest skirt and even – was he joking? – to leave your knickers off, but you were determined to dress in keeping with your new status. You bought a cream cashmere two-piece and a midnight-blue silk blouse: you even laid off the make-up and carried an attaché case – although there was nothing in it. They weren't happy at the run-through – the producer put an arm around your shoulders: 'No need to be so formal'. Thereafter you just came straight in from the clubs: they all really went for that.

'Keep smiling,' said the producer, 'and only say nice things – leave the hard analysis to the boys.' But you couldn't see that there was anything to summarize or be remotely expert about. Before the race you'd all say that the fastest would win, then watch as the fastest won, and then afterwards confirm that the fastest had indeed won. Swimming wasn't like athletics, it had no tactics: they could only swim as fast as they could – do their time, do their time – and if that didn't work there was no Plan B. It struck you again how stupid it looked – such ugly splashings about! – and how different from the way it had felt while you were doing it.

The action replays were excruciating: what was the point in showing the audience what they'd just seen, over and over again, from every conceivable angle? It was as if they were hoping for a different outcome or that time could be reversed so that we could have another go or – with the rare British triumphs – to try to prolong the moment, to hold it forever.

Your function seemed to be to bring luck, like a touchstone, or even – as if you were a magician – to exert some influence on events. One of the guys joked that you should be praying, burning incense or sacrificing a sheep. Most of your fellow-pundits, though, affected a condescending air, implying that the only reason they weren't still trouncing those epigones in the pool was that they now had better things to do. The smug presenter seemed to be under the impression that he was making it all happen, and that, like Prospero, he had only to clap his hands for everything to disappear. You felt that they were more like dead souls tuning in from purgatory, incorporeal and powerless, able only to watch and envy.

On Finals Day you watched and envied as a fifteen-year-old from Ongar smashed your British and Commonwealth record, won the gold, took your title. Dawn: you could faintly recollect her – she never spoke and looked through you as if you were invisible. She still had that same amorphous, unfinished look, like a tadpole. As the studio ritually exulted, you kept watching the monitor: you saw her eyes seeking the camera, then felt a jolt as they locked on to yours, felt the voltage of her triumph pass through you. Somehow you knew that it was you – not her mum and dad or Coach – who was in her mind at that moment: you thought you could hear a little voice saying, with incomprehensible hatred, 'That's finished you, Psycho.' You'd never thought of the previous record-holder – you couldn't even remember her name – but now you wondered how she'd been feeling four years ago. And Karen, if she'd been watching in the madhouse? You became aware that you were speaking: 'This is another great day for British swimming!' You didn't feel very patriotic: it was as if you were being asked to compliment the rope technique of someone who'd just hung you.

Afterwards, you ran to the car park. You wildly cursed Fish Two as it inched through the mid-morning traffic, tormented by the fear that your medals would be gone – crumbled to dust or removed by ASA agents for presentation to Dawn. Home at last, you closed the curtains and then placed the gold, still surprisingly heavy and as bright as ever, around your neck – slowly and reverently, as if you were bestowing it on yourself.

When the calendar appeared, your face was indeed well-hidden, but your name was on the photograph, along with a full list of titles and records. The sand logo had somehow dropped off, and the thong had either been lost in shadow or airbrushed out – your bum appeared like twin moons glowing with unearthly light. In the angle of arm and back, the penumbra of one breast was visible with, beyond the areola's dark crenellation, the nipple, like a tiny silver flare. You didn't like the back of your head: the pale hair was like an exploding magnesium mask, behind which you imagined your face disfigured or erased. The other eleven months were also ex-athletes, their features similarly obscured, their bodies – all in tasteful black-and-white – like undulating landscapes on which seismic shifts were extruding knolls of breasts and buttocks. 'I told you it would be artistic,' said Coach, but all you could see were twelve women who, for all their efforts and achievements, had finally been reduced to what – according to another of his favourite maxims – it all came down to: 'Tits and ass . . . or sometimes ass and tits'.

Once again your date-book was full of photo-sessions: you walked in, they told you to get your kit off, you walked straight out again. Coach was furious: 'You don't understand! These are top whack, Little Mandy rates!' A newspaper had started a series, 'Countdown To Ecstasy', in which each day schoolgirl Mandy would wear less and less until at last on her sixteenth birthday – although she already looked twice that age – all would be revealed. The morning headline had been: 'WE'RE ALL SO PROUD OF MANDY – HEAD-MISTRESS SAYS'. You weren't flattered by the comparison. Coach couldn't grasp that it wasn't about money or prud-ishness, but that you felt that something terrible would happen to you: that all your past would be retrospectively reduced to tits and ass and ass and tits peek-a-booing up and down a pool – and without a past how could you have a present, let alone a future? Two weeks went by with no work and no calls. You pushed yourself ever harder in the gym: soon your body wouldn't need to say no because no one would dare to ask it the question. You thought of yourself as being in train-ing to clean-jerk the whole world – but you wouldn't take it on your shoulders like Atlas, just bounce it a few times like a goalkeeper before giving it a good boot into infinity. You knew it might be difficult, but at least it gave you a target beyond mere fitness or fantasy. You were wearing your gold medal all the time now. Nobody on the streets could possibly suspect that it was around your neck: its weight made you feel potent and dangerous, as if you were carrying a bomb which you might at any moment choose to detonate.

At last Coach rang and invited you to lunch in Soho: he sounded strangely solemn – the familiar spiel about big breaks and golden opportunities lacked its customary interpolated yips and yells. When you got there he was already into a second bottle of wine. Two waiters were dragging over a third seat, of heavy, carved wood with padded armrests, a cross between a baby's highchair and a throne. You followed their gaze towards the door, but no grand entrance ensued. On turning back, however, you saw that the place had been occupied by an enormously fat man, his chins and jowls vibrating, as if from the impact of being dropped from a great height – you automatically looked up for a hole in the ceiling or in the sky. He shook your hand: 'I've always admired your work.' You must have looked confused – 'Well, isn't swimming work? To do anything well you have to have worked at it. Hard. Like drinking' – he drained Coach's glass and waved on another bottle – 'or smoking' – he lit a stogey, blew himself a large blue halo, then stubbed it out and replaced it in his top pocket – 'even breathing' – he exhaled mightily for a full half-minute and then opened the menu. He never did order: presumably the waiters knew that he was having the usual – which, when it arrived, appeared to be large helpings of everything.

Coach's introduction wasn't necessary. You'd often seen him: he was impossible to miss. Camel-hair coat draped over his shoulders, eyes masked by bamboo-framed, square-lensed shades, his massive frame shaking at some private joke, he would coast through Fitzrovia and Soho, although his businesses had long since moved out of the area. When people stepped out of his way he would confront them in the gutter. The Porn King, The Sultan Of Sleaze, Percy Filth – he had as many nicknames as a swimmer, but he'd always made you think of The Fat Controller in *Thomas the Tank Engine*. Now you were fascinated to see that – although he was said to be one of the richest men in Britain – he chose to wear a wig that seemed to have been moulded from grey plastic.

'I'm told that you have delicate sensibilities,' he said. 'I consider that to be a prerequisite for our line of work. It's a spiritual thing: punters want madonnas, saints, fallen angels who'll dive down deep into their filth, give them a good see-ing-to and then haul them up to paradise where even sexier angels will give them even better seeings-to forever and ever. Amen.'

'Tits and ass. Ass and tits,' put in Coach. 'It's what makes the world go round.'

'The universe and infinity, too. Alas,' said The Fat Man. You weren't frightened or offended: his silly Satan act just made you laugh. Dad would have wiped the floor with him: he'd have known which books and films the lines were nicked from, which half-forgotten B-movie actor's mannerisms were being copied – you could make a start with Bogart's rival club owner in *Casablanca*. A fat man might be able to control things, but he could never be sinister. 'I am also an admirer of your work in the smiling field,' he said, clinking glasses with you.

'It'll be hard work: films, live appearances, the odd one-off special – but you won't have to do anything you don't want to do. No animals. And there's no pimps or rough stuff these days, just tax returns and charity work. We'll play up the swimming angle at first: poolside frolics, subaqua sex, naughty dolphins, water sports . . . Have you still got your medals?'

You felt the secret throb of the gold, slotted sideways between your breasts: 'No,' you said.

'We can get replicas. We'll feature those as well . . . The Golden Cherry . . . The Olympic Ring . . .' He produced another cigar stub and made as if to write with it, then comically double-took and after much pocket-patting – ignoring Coach's flourished Parker – came up with a leaking Biro. He scribbled furiously on the menu and then pushed it over to you. 'Keep it,' he said, 'that's your contract.' The figure made your previous earnings – even the milk and catalogues – look like nothing. 'And that's the bottom line. You could double it. And there's a contributory pension scheme: it's a career – a job for life, if you want. It's my ex-models that run the organization now. They edit all the magazines. One's my chief accountant: I put her through business college – mind like a steel trap. I'm like a father to all my girls – eventually.'

Coach was staring at the menu: you'd always been impressed by his ability to read things upside down. He didn't so much as blink as you slowly tipped your couscous over his head. And neither of them tried to stop you from dashing the wine in their faces, as if they'd been anticipating such a resolution. You walked out to the sound of The Fat Man's laughter and Coach saying – in the resigned tones of a surgeon who'd just lost a patient – 'Why can't she understand that she's just another cunt?'

When you were back outside on the street, weird-looking men converged on you as usual, like filings flying to a magnet. Fish Two was back in Chelsea, all the cabs were taken, so you ducked into the tube station. If you couldn't fly away at least you could go underground. A train was in, as if waiting for you, its rear carriage blissfully empty until a man hurtled through the closing doors, lurched towards you, then slumped down opposite. He was panting heavily and his black hair glistened with sweat or oil: you could see vermiculations of white scalp beneath. He looked familiar, but you had no idea where from: these days you were forgetting most of the faces and all of the names. He took out a gold propelling-pencil and, without taking his eyes off you, began to scribble furiously in a creased red Silvine notebook. He wasn't bad-looking – thirtyish, thin-faced with wire glasses, but the set of his body suggested that he'd been working out. Could he have been among your one-night stands? You stared fiercely back until he blinked: it was like a Venus flytrap closing – his eyelashes were incredibly long. Now you knew: he'd been at the next table in the restaurant, alone, with a stack of books, from which he read in turn like Dad used to do. You'd noticed him because he hadn't been noticing you. He seemed to have left his books behind.

When you changed lines at Embankment he followed you, still panting, still writing. As you felt the approaching train's rush of air on your face, you guessed what was happening. He was The Fat Controller's bodyguard, deputed to follow and punish you, and he was about to push you on to the rails. You fought desperately through the crowd, down the platform: he followed, but you boarded safely. A packed aisle separated you, but you could still feel his eyes boring into your back. At Sloane Square you waited until you were masked by people entering, then slipped out. You ran half-way up the escalator before you looked back to confirm that you'd finally lost him.

You weren't fifty yards down the King's Road when he drew level with you, running sideways. He informed you that you were a goddess, his muse – only he pronounced it 'moose' – and that you'd inspired him to write this poem. You stopped and he circled you as he read:

> *'I don the Nessus-shirt of your loveliness*
> *As your cool regard puts Mammon to the knife.*
> *No peace on earth for the beauty of holiness:*
> *Dis-wards I track you, Eurydice, beloved wife . . .'*

Well, it made a change from 'Shall I compare thee to a summer's day?', but you knew that it wasn't any good because Dad had always said that – regrettably – real poetry these days couldn't rhyme. And you knew that this couldn't be the man you were waiting for because he wouldn't have to rabbit on so – when your eyes met all words would become redundant. The poet's trembling fingers moved towards your face, but you jerked back: your man wouldn't need to touch you either – no talking, no touching, you'd just merge. You noticed that he wasn't reading from the notebook, but reciting the poem perfectly, from memory: it had probably been written years ago, to be ready if he should ever see a blonde in a red dress throwing a glass of wine over a fat man.

'Skin flayed, albedo soot-grimed, back from the grave,
Darker mistress, to harm and heal, to slay and save.'

'I don't need saving,' you interrupted.

'No,' he said testily, 'she's going to save him. You're going to save me.'

' 'Scuse me miss, but is this man bothering you?' – A shaven head interposed itself: on the craning neck you could descry the letters WHU and a dripping dagger in ink and pin tattoos. You'd seen this one before as well: he'd clocked you at the ticket barrier and now, after following, was posing as a passing knight errant. They began to bristle and growl at each other like dogs – with you, the disputed bone between them, suddenly forgotten. You knew men: it would take them ages to work themselves up to it – their foreplay for fighting was more elaborate and probably more tender than for sex. At this moment, in a nimbus of furs – the skins of specially-bred marl-grey leopards with symmetrical spots – Diana Ross walked by. She cleaved the air like a ship's figurehead, her hair blown straight back by her own personal gale, just like in her videos. She *was* a goddess: serene, untroubled, she smiled at you and, raising one pencilled eyebrow, said something you didn't catch. The poet had just got in the first shoulder-shove and his rival was looking distinctly apprehensive. You guessed that the poet would beat up the thug, who would then write a great poem about it. You left them to each other and followed Diana, but she had already disappeared. There was no sign of her in the shops: although it seemed unlikely, you even checked in the Chelsea Barracks. You'd known that she was in London – you had a ticket to see her at Wembley Arena next week – but decided that it must have been a vision, a sign sent to you, at this darkest moment, that everything was still going to be all right.

I I I

COACH NEVER RANG YOU AGAIN. Three weeks later he sent you a cheque for outstanding balance of earnings, with heavy deductions for dry-cleaning bills and that final lunch, for which an itemized tab was enclosed – after you'd left, he and The Fat Controller had got through four more bottles of retsina and half a dozen limoncellos. By now you were so busy – driving, working out, shopping – that you didn't know how you'd ever managed to fit in anything else. The last four years had at least bought you the time to relax, to think about the future: you sent off for college prospectuses, but never got round to reading them. You'd embarked on a new intensive fitness programme of rowing, stepping, boxercising, tanning and toning – although you ignored the nutritional regime because eating just made you constipated and you somehow felt that if you were really fit you shouldn't need food. You ran at least twelve miles a day, and were thinking of entering the London Marathon: there was no effort involved – it was as if you were lifting your feet to allow the pavement to move. You felt like you had two bodies: one was super-fit, but the other remained an aggregation of stubborn aches and pains. You seemed to occupy both at the same time: you looked in the mirror, but could see no difference – there was still only one of you. Sometimes you wondered if exercise was a form of giving birth, as if you were generating a series of separate selves – physically perfect, but soulless, invisible. At home or in company you were increasingly restless – feeling that you should be somewhere else. When you were in, you wanted out, but then immediately wanted back in again. The gym was the only place in which you could relax: at once part of the world, aware of the sound and motion of others around you, and beyond it, cocooned inside your own exertions. And all the men there ignored you: either they were gay or narciss-ism had smothered their sex-drives.

You'd already signed up for more work with the oil company, making a last TV ad – in a near-subliminal flash, parodying the old milk poster, swigging a bottle of lube – and paying a publicity visit to one of the North Sea rigs. It was like a maximum security unit for psychopaths and rapists: unlike the sailors, the wild seas seemed only to have brutalized them. You were black and blue from their pinching fingers: they stared hungrily into your face, as if seeking the answer to some crucial question. The calendar – open in March at your May picture – was on every bulkhead, with your absurd luminous bottom feathered and pitted by darts. 'I don't know much about art,' said a man in a hard hat, taking aim, 'but I know what I like.' Afterwards the firm offered you a contract for two years of similar gigs: 'The Golden Girl Ambassadress' they were going to call you – they were shocked when you declined.

You gave up clubbing. You still believed in Mr Right, but now he'd have to come to you. Sometimes you'd lie on your bed, staring at the skylight, imagining him parachuting through. At night you danced alone to Diana Ross or watched your favourite videos – especially *Love Story* – again and again. You were beginning to think that Jennifer had done the sensible thing by dying young, while she was still loved, while she still knew all the Mozart Köchel numbers – whatever they might be. You bought *Oliver's Story*, but it was the wrong sequel – you didn't care about him, just wanted to know how Jenny was getting on in heaven. You were drinking more, too: as a joke you kept your booze in the bathroom, with a bottle of gin in the cistern in case Mum and Dad ever came to call.

Then Coach rang: First Coach, the original. You'd gone ex-directory, so he must have got the number from Coach Two. He said that he'd just left his wife because he realized he'd always loved you – but you knew from the papers that she'd found his defloration diaries and photo collection, kicked him out and gone to the press. A series of calls – sobbing or silent – followed. You left the receiver off the hook, but he had your address too: he started ringing your bell and shouting pleas and threats into the entry-phone. One night he even got into the hall and tapped a soft four-beat tattoo on your door for what seemed like hours. You hid your head under the pillows until he'd gone. Then the sound began again

– at the window this time: had he climbed a ladder or was he hovering there like a vampire bat? You finally summoned the courage to open the curtains: it was only four large moths, throwing themselves into the glass. They kept it up all night, even after you'd turned out the lights.

Leaving for the gym next morning you discovered Coach crouching behind Fish Two. You hardly knew him: he looked twenty years older and was wearing a ridiculous shaggy orange wig. Perhaps it was a disguise – or did he and The Fat Controller both operate on the assumption that if you wore something that looked artificial everyone would believe it must be real? He stretched out his arms towards you. 'Don't worry,' you said, 'the future is a straight line. So you can go and sweep out the crater of Etna, Mr Grimes.'

He obviously hadn't read *The Water Babies*: 'You're as mad as Karen,' he yelled, as you drove away. 'Fucking butterfly!'

He didn't come back and whenever your phone did ring it was always other men who claimed to have known you. After a while, though, you increasingly often returned home to find no messages, and almost felt that you'd have been glad of even them. Sometimes in the long, silent nights, you half-wished that the moths would come back. Apart from prospectuses and bills, your only correspondence was from Newcastle, forwarded by Coach Two. You opened it out of boredom, to find that the former obscenities had given way to family gossip, descriptions of the weather, news of their small successes and disappointments, confidings of their hopes and fears. They even signed them now and included their addresses, begging you to reply. All they'd really wanted was a pen pal. At about this time you stopped seeing Mum and Dad, telling them that you were going abroad on assignments: the last time you'd visited there had been a terrible smell in the living room, as if one or both had fouled themselves.

You hung around the gym all day – first in, last out. One evening, as you were sitting in the bar for the final half hour, pretending to read your prospectuses – in which the same girl in a white dress seemed to be standing outside every Hall of Residence – one of the gays came over. If you'd ever known his name you'd forgotten it. 'Pardon me,' – he gestured at your cleavage and smiled with a sound like a sword being unsheathed – 'but we were wondering – what exactly did you win your gold medal for?'

You were flustered: 'Flying,' then – 'butterflying.'

'Oh, was that it?' he said. 'We thought it might have been for gracefulness. Or beauty.' He took your hand and lowered his head: you felt his lips buss just above your wrist, in a light but firm contact – like a passport being stamped as you enter a new country. As he rejoined his friends you wondered if you'd been the butt of some cruel, subtle joke – they all hated women, didn't they? – but none of them was laughing. They raised their glasses and gravely toasted you. Perhaps this explained the kindness of the sailors: it looked as if your man, when he arrived, might have to be gay.

On leaving, you were still full of energy, which even two hours' driving – left-right then right-left – didn't release. You couldn't even lose yourself any more: although you seldom recognized anything, you always knew where you were. Fish Two had begun to handle oddly – sometimes responding sluggishly, at others seeming to start turning in advance of the wheel. For a while it toiled along a flat, featureless road as if climbing a steep hill, then went light, as if freewheeling down the far side. Suddenly it aquaplaned – on a bone-dry surface – to shoot a red light, then cut up a patrol car – the occupants mercifully didn't react, as if they hadn't believed their eyes. When you tried to slow down, Fish Two wanted to speed up: the pedals kept playfully switching functions. Back home – after it had taken you three attempts to park in your usual space – you slapped its bonnet lightly – then as hard as you could. 'I hope you get stolen,' you said, leaving its alarms unset. You'd never liked it as much as Fish One: maybe it was time for Fish Three?

Although you'd planned to sit and watch *Love Story*, you knew that you'd have to dance for a good while to sufficiently tire yourself. Your body felt to be vibrating, with a noise like a generator hum, and the hand searching for your doorkeys seemed to be glowing like the calendar bum. As usual, the second Yale was awkward, refusing to fit its lock, but tonight neither blowing on it nor rubbing it against your hip did the trick. The ground floor and basement lights were on, but you didn't ring their bells: although you couldn't recall who lived there, you feared that they'd only try to force their lusts or loneliness upon you. The white glow pulsed, the humming got louder, your nerve ends screamed: you had to do something before you exploded . . . You rammed your Head bag behind the dustbins and with wild exhilaration, in your short red velvet dress and high heels, you began to run.

As you glided down Tite Street towards the river anyone looking through their curtains would have taken you for an apparition. Running like this was even more comfortable than in shorts and trainers: you pictured yourself winning the marathon – dressed to kill, hair immaculate, in full war paint, leaving all those miserable athletes sweating and cursing in your wake. You crossed a bridge that you didn't recognize: neither the Albert nor the Chelsea, this one was narrow, unlit and strangely sticky underfoot. No traffic passed: it seemed to stretch forever, as if it were spanning the Amazon, not the silly old Thames. The structure shook: you could hear great waves crashing and breaking against it. The far shore, when you finally reached it, was lined with dark houses: although you looked left and right, Battersea Park had disappeared.

You ran on and on: no longer aimlessly left-right or right-left, but unerringly straight. The moon came and went in various phases in different parts of the sky, until the clouds parted to reveal that it had split into two well-separated halves. You saw a sign pointing to Tooting but, recalling your hated school nickname, decided not to follow it. These were parts of London you'd never visited. 'The cream rises to the top,' Coach Two liked to say – for him High Barnet was the last stop before heaven – 'and the scum settles south of the river.' In fact, it seemed to be uninhabited, but as you were concentrating on your feet and the moons, padding along together, you'd only have noticed people if you'd stepped on them or if they'd been falling out of the sky. There was another sign – to Crystal Palace, this time – but you ignored it too. You needed more than an Olympic-size pool: an instinct was drawing you onwards, lemming-like, towards the coast, to Worthing. When you reached it you were going to run past the fences and DANGER signs and head straight over the cliff-edge. You imagined the sea below, readying itself to welcome you back ... but it was going to be disappointed, as you spiralled upwards, waving it a fond farewell, into the grey sky, the true welkin.

Were lemmings small and furry? What kind of sound would they make? You settled, as you ran on, for a mouse-like squeaking. You decided that you should practise flying on the way, so you started to spear-dive: although you always crashed to the ground, you could feel yourself hanging in the air for a little longer each time. Flying was evidently going to need even more than Coach's 110%, but at least you knew the secret: someone had told you that you hadn't to move your arms, just let it all come from the hips. The falls must have cut your head: your hair felt matted with warm jam – but maybe it wasn't blood because it smelt of chlorine and tasted of semen . . . and, besides, the stains on your dress were black. The twin moons had gone, but now something else seemed to be wrong with the sky. A grey smear appeared and then faded in three false dawns before you were relieved to see the sun peeping over the rooftops like a chad. But then, to its right, a second sun appeared, to be followed by yet another, smaller one below. They rose as a triangle: Mum, Dad and Baby suns.

Then a voice spoke to you, rattling and booming as if it was issuing from a cheap speaker-cabinet, reminiscent of Coach One and Two, but with a mid-Atlantic accent: it could only be God. 'Take all thou hast and give it to the poor!' So you pressed your credit cards on two terrified schoolboys at a bus stop, insisting that they wrote down your cash PINS. To an elderly black woman with bowing, swollen legs you gave your watch and rings: you wanted her to have your car and flat too, but the keys, still clutched in your hand, seemed to have part-melted and fused. It was at this moment that you realized that you'd gone mad, for Diana Ross's huge, vivid eyes were blazing out from under her headscarf. You ran on into a small park. On the far side of a stagnant, mossy lake, a ragged man was lying under a polythene sheet. As you approached, he raised himself up: his hair and beard seemed to be growing sideways, as if he'd wrapped his face in a weft of raw, dusty wool. He bowed his head and without pausing or even breaking stride, you hung your medal around his neck. 'Ta, love,' he said complacently, in an accent you couldn't place. When people asked him what he'd won his medal for, what would his answer be?

And then God spoke again: 'Humble thyself! Roll on the ground!' And so you did, self-consciously wriggling your limbs like an overturned beetle. 'Eat the dirt!' God said. So you ate the dirt – it tasted like dirt. 'Eat that worm!': it tasted of nothing, but afterwards you could feel the bits seeking each other inside you. And then God said, 'Take off all your clothes and walk naked among the traffic!'

And you said, 'Piss off! Typical bloody man!'

God didn't waste any more words on you. The three suns moved in close overhead, holding you in their arc-lamp dazzle until, with a blare of sirens, His policemen arrived to take you away. You were sure that they were the same two who had haunted you and Dad at Waterloo: at any rate, the uniforms were identical. They seemed to be in no hurry to get you back to the station: you passed the park three times – they were taking the scenic route. Although you were dirty and bloody, sobbing and trying to retch up the worm that was thriving on your stomach acids, you were just another cunt to them. The one in the back's hands – the right up your dress, the left down – burrowed frantically towards each other, while he sucked at your earlobe like a badly-weaned kitten. Then the driver pulled into the kerb and they switched. This one tried to force your head down to his lap: there was a smell of cheese – you shut your eyes. 'You're worse than a fucking animal,' he kept muttering, while his mate did farmyard impressions. A second pair of hands seemed to be busying themselves about your body – he must have kicked off his size twelves and got stuck in with his feet, monkey-style.

When you finally reached the bridewell they stopped touching you, although the way everyone was staring felt nearly as bad. You were searched by Dawn, dressed as a WPC – but you knew that it wasn't really her because this one could at least giggle. The subsequent interview, conducted by two men in horrible orange leather jackets like on 'The Sweeney', was baffling. Why did they bother asking questions if they weren't going to believe any of the answers? 'Who's been hitting you? Your pimp? A punter?' Life for them was so simple: if they were the police then you could only be a victim or a criminal. For next of kin you gave them Coach Two: your parents, you said, were dead. One went to check out your address and telephone number: when he returned he acted as if his having heard your voice on the recorded message proved that you couldn't be here. They seemed to think you were a thief – 'What have you taken?' they kept asking – but how could that be when you'd been giving things away?

'I won that medal,' you said, 'so why can't I do what I like with it?'

When you told them you were going to Worthing, one said, 'What thing?' and the other, 'What war?' If you were mad then they were madder: 'Do you have any proof of your identity?' – that was the sort of thing Dad now spent his days mulling over.

When you remained silent they started shouting, but when you did answer – 'Promo-ing,' when asked about your job – they liked that even less. 'It's in the dictionary,' you told them, 'along with welkin.'

They went out and left you alone with Dawn for a while: her giggling relaxed you like a gently running stream – you closed your eyes, you even nodded off. 'Manic.' A man in a braided cap was standing over you. 'You can tell by the pupils. Like pinpricks. And there' – he sniffed – 'off the skin and breath. Unmistakable. The sweet smell of psychosis. Go on' – he urged the others – 'so you'll know it again.' They all inhaled, savoured it for ten seconds and then, in unison, breathed out. 'We'll pack her off to hospital for X-rays,' he said, gently helping you to your feet, 'and let them have the bloody paperwork!' You were lowered into a chair in the corridor: a hand gave you a mug of tea, but another immediately snatched it away: 'Head wound! No fluids!'

'Spoilsport,' said the desk sergeant, pretending to zip up his fly.

As you waited you heard someone say, 'Model. Used to be a swimmer. Shame.' Everyone stopped to look at you, presumably under instructions to observe your pupils and smell your breath. You could see the fear and hatred in their eyes: it was as if you'd committed the worst of crimes – as if you'd been given a magic lamp and rubbed it for beauty and fame but then, as your third wish, chosen madness. There ought to be a law against it, they were thinking – there ought to be a law against everything. As the ambulancemen were wheeling you away, one of the coppers who'd brought you in, smiling sweetly, opened his fist to reveal your medal in his palm. When people asked him what he'd won it for, what would his answer be?

No sooner were you in your hospital bed than a face was thrust close to yours. It was Dawn again, this time in a nurse's outfit. 'We hate people like you' – she was hissing like a fuse – 'wasting our time when there are really sick patients who need us.' Five minutes later she was back, all smiles: 'Sorry! They told me you were the overdose!' However, after you'd run out of the ward and she'd had to chase and drag you back, she delivered her first speech again. Your wrist itched and ached around the drip: she called it a 'butterfly' – you thought that was a bad joke. When you'd torn it out for the third time she strapped down your arms and reinserted the needle with the same venom which the man on the rig had bullseyed your calendar shot. Sedated, you couldn't remember much after that, only a pinkish glow from which a soft voice periodically issued. It asked even dafter questions than the police: Who is the Prime Minister? What is The Queen's name? – You couldn't remember, but began instead to relate how you'd met them, only for it to interrupt with the request that you count up to ten. To spite it, you counted down instead.

Although you'd not been aware of visitors, some of your things had appeared: it was nice to have your drop-headed toothbrush and fluffy white bathrobe, but the starchy institution nightdress continued to chafe you – the nurse had deemed yours to be too short. You'd feared what your compact mirror might reveal, but your face was unmarked, even the scalp cut that had bled so profusely was tiny and already almost healed. Your pupils looked to be their normal size. Could your hair have gone white under the silver? It was somehow more disturbing that you looked exactly the same. Even your make-up had survived intact: the skin was thoroughly lacquered. You discovered that Dad's *Buddenbrooks* was on the bedside table: you weren't about to read that now – you donated it to the hospital library.

The youngest doctor watched you intently as he moved around the ward, but would always try to mask his face with his clipboard when he neared your bed. His gaze was drawn to the frayed vent in the left side of your gown, through which the golden line of your hip protruded: he forced his eyes away again and again, but they always slid back. He was one of those men that you knew you should find attractive but didn't, except when he went nearly strabismic under the strain. Had he watched you win your gold? Or had he seen the silver bottom? You couldn't take in what he was saying, but you knew it would only amount to the usual 'medical science confesses itself baffled'. You could tell by his reactions that sometimes you were unconsciously speaking your thoughts aloud, while at others not saying anything when you thought you had. The best policy seemed to be total silence and thinking as little as possible: soon you found that you were able to block out his voice altogether, although his lips continued to move. One night you awoke to see him standing next to you and, as you watched, a bewildering range of emotions – from tenderness to loathing – flitted like time-lapsed clouds across his face. How horrible it was that you, by just lying there, could make him feel such things!

All tests and X-rays were clear: you were being discharged. You imagined that they would take you back to the park where the police had picked you up: because the drugs had converted your energy to inertia, you'd already decided not to carry on to Worthing, but to jog back to Chelsea and rest up for a couple of days before setting out again. Then you felt the doctor's hands firmly gripping your shoulders. He was obviously speaking with great emphasis, his mouth repeating the same shapes – so you tuned back in to listen. 'You're going to The Retreat' – for the first time his eyes, filled with tears, looked into yours – 'you'll be safe there.' Why did everyone want either to hurt or protect you?

Even before the ambulance stopped you somehow knew

that it was taking you back to your old school. Time had not been kind to it: the winds had blown the towers away and levelled the roofs and had begun to uncover streaks of honey-coloured sandstone beneath the grime. The extensions had been painted primrose and joined to form a long single strip: most of the windows had disappeared. The sports facilities were also in decline: there was no sign of the track and pool and only the tennis court, covered with last autumn's rotting leaves, remained. You felt guilty that you hadn't kept up your subscription to the Old Girls' Association.

Inside the main entrance you were confronted by a woman wearing rolled-down stockings and a back-to-front housecoat tightly fastened with a triple knot. She reminded you of Karen – that is, if she'd seen no sunlight for the last decade and had done nothing but eat. 'You-you-you-you-you-you-you,' she began, wagging an arthritic-looking finger in your face – but the anticipated stream of insulting nouns and adjectives never followed. 'You-you-you-you-you-you-you:' she did the same to the nurse who was putting her arm around your shoulders, then to the space that you'd both vacated – when you looked back she was remonstrating with a painting of a vase of flowers. The smiling nurse limped down the corridor: you realized that you'd begun to limp too, in sympathy. The entire left side of her body seemed to be dying or dead, but it didn't seem to have embittered her – maybe it was even the secret of her cheerfulness? 'Is this a madhouse?' you asked, and she hugged you to her, shaking with mirth, as if this were the most ridiculous thing she'd ever heard.

'Of course not,' she said, 'this is The Retreat.'

And as she showed you round you understood that the house itself, solid and perfectly aligned, was indeed sane: it was the residents – or 'ressies' as she called them – who were mad. They all wore clothes that were somehow at once stiff and shapeless, with the colours all run together: now you knew who'd bought all the stuff in your first catalogue. You wondered if they were all former swimmers and athletes sent here to acquire the new skills needed to survive in the wider world. One elderly man was practising running sideways: maybe the poet had learnt that in here? Others were aspiring to flight, but eagles and chickens, rather than butterflies, seemed to be the favoured models: although they appeared oblivious to one another, they must have been well-choreographed, for they never collided. You watched a game of ping-pong: it was like a film with frames missing – one player finally crawled under the table after the ball and never reappeared. There was silence as you approached the ward, but all hell broke loose when you reached the door. Although no one looked in your direction you knew that the banging and howling was for you: the disturbance spread across the room like ripples from a diver entering water. You walked straight back out: even here you weren't going to fit in – you were mad in the wrong kind of way.

The corridor's walls and ceiling were the same shade of grey as the ressies' faces. There was something reassuring, oddly familiar about it. As the nurse looked on benevolently, you walked back to the far end and then carefully paced it out. It was, as you'd suspected, the length of a competition pool, exactly fifty metres. You backed against the wall and stared down the corridor as if it were your lane: out of an expectant silence you heard once more the mysterious susurration of calm water, saw the black-and-white linoleum tiles begin to shimmer and distort. Without waiting for the starter's signal, you launched yourself forward.

It wasn't exactly like swimming – or even running, or dancing, or flying. The element you moved through didn't feel like water or air. You weren't aware of going through the two sets of Perspex fire doors so maybe you'd gone underground and were tunnelling like a mole. You touched on the emergency exit's rail and twist-turned, realizing that your nose was dripping claret for the first time in years. On your fourth and final lap the silver fog once again greeted you. 'No pain, no gain,' you gritted, but this was the worst ever – it felt as if you were twisting in flames. Then, just as before, you heard the sound of the crowd – there were no identifiable voices this time, just a general roar that lifted you and carried you to the finish. You saw that every doorway was filled with cheering faces and applauding hands. Although there was no Tannoy, you knew that you'd not only won but smashed the record. Nurse presented your prize – not a medal this time, but two pale yellow capsules chased down by a beaker of syrupy water – and then, towelling the blood from your face, led you away. Unlike Mum's, her laughter was kind. The ressies were softly patting and stroking you as you passed: your golden skin and shining hair notwithstanding, they were welcoming you into their grey world.

'New places are always exciting, aren't they?' said Nurse, 'so let's have a little rest before we see the doctors.' Producing a massive bunch of keys she unlocked a door marked in large red letters SAFE ROOM. It was unfurnished, except for a stack of cushions and beanbags in the middle and a thick springy carpet which appeared to have spread to climb the walls like moss. There was no window: the only light source was a low wattage bulb set behind a grille in the ceiling. Just as a mad-house had become a retreat and its inmates ressies, so a padded cell was now a safe room. Nurse had vanished: you didn't know whether she'd locked you in because you couldn't find the door again. There wasn't even a peephole, although you sensed that you were being observed.

Your adrenaline was still pumping: the carpet felt like a trampoline and when you jumped, your fingers only just failed to reach the ceiling. As you circled the room you felt as if you were in zero gravity, beginning to float: you flung yourself at a wall, expecting that it would engulf you like a vertical feather bed, only to crumple half-stunned from the force of the

impact. The Safe Room, you now understood, was designed
to be safe not for you but from you: although the padding
ensured that you couldn't damage it, you could still hurt yourself. These walls might not have smashed records or met The
Queen or stripped off for calendars, but – by interposing
themselves between the mad and the sane – they were of
infinitely greater account than you. And they would still be
standing long after you and your medals were gone and forgotten.

Cold and shivering, you crawled over to the cushions. The
drugs didn't seem to be working – or at any rate you were
still conscious. Beyond your agitated breathing and heartbeat
there were two strange noises – a high whine and a low hum.
It was like Dad's account of being in an anechoic chamber,
in which he'd been able to listen to his own nervous system
and circulating blood: you began to marvel, but then both
sounds stopped simultaneously. The light above you flared,
then dimmed. There was no wall-switch: someone must have
been adjusting it in the corridor. It began violently flickering.
You wondered if they were testing you for epilepsy: one night,
in a club, you'd watched as strobes had triggered a *grand mal*

fit in a man who'd been pestering you – at first you'd thought it was your sarcasm that had done it.

Now, dreading darkness, you glared into the light and gradually willed the flashing to a stop, then held it steady at its previous level. You knew that if you looked away or blinked then it would begin again. After a while you saw that there was no longer a bulb behind the grille but a single eye: as blank as Dawn's, with a china-blue iris and hugely dilated pupil, it was staring you out. Finally its lid slowly closed, with an audible click, then opened, only to wink again, and again, faster and faster until it disappeared inside the intensifying flicker.

It seemed as if twin rotor blades were sucking up the light and, in a shower of silver-blue sparks, chopping it to pieces, which they then extruded as slowly falling flakes, like plaster or snow. One of these – like a scrap of burnt paper or a withered leaf – landed on your right wrist. It was only when you saw it quivering that you realized it was a tiny brown butterfly. A second alighted, facing it – then two more, above and below, interlocking to form a rough circle. Then you heard a voice, loud and slightly distorted – not God's this time, but Dad's. '*Lasiommata megera*,' he said, 'the Wall Brown. Basks in the sun. Is nervous and easily disturbed.' More and more were fluttering down to you, their joined fours overlapping each other like scales, until they had entirely covered your needle-bruised and swollen arm, easing the pain like a poultice. You saw that others had simultaneously enwrapped the left, from fingertips to shoulder.

'*Lysandra coridon*,' said Dad. Chalkhill Blues were now dappling your feet and shins. '*Vanessa atalanta:*' even though he had grown to twice his previous size, you recognized the Red Admiral from your garden as, followed by his crew, he proudly took up his former position on your patella. '*Leptidea sinapis:*' a cluster of Woodwhites formed the shape of an eye-holed mask that fitted over your face, while '*Gonepteryx rhamni*' – Brimstones – similarly encased your head, returning your hair to something like its natural colour. 'The Fritillaries . . . the Speckled Woods . . . the Mountain Ringlets:' Dad had started speaking in his Seamus Android voice, as if these imagos were long-lost friends and relations being summoned to 'This Is Your Life', filling up all the empty pages of the big red book.

'*Pieris brassicae*:' a swarm of Cabbage Whites fastened on
the wall that had hurt you and began munching at it – the
room was no longer quite so safe. In great showers, like con-
fetti, the butterflies kept flooding out of the light, becoming
progressively larger and more beautiful: Emperors, Kings and
Queens – how could they be getting through such a small
aperture? A rippling quilt now covered and warmed your
body: a wedge of *Clossiana freija* even replaced the cushion,
to give your head a softer rest. '*Inachis io*,' said Dad as
Seamus, 'the Peacock,' as the last two – huge russets, goggle-
eyed – hinged over your right breast.

The flickering stopped, leaving the ceiling wreathed in its
former pearl-grey light. Apart from the sound of the Whites
eating the Safe Room, there was silence. Then you saw that
something was moving around behind the grille: not the eye,
but an enormous trapped butterfly. Far too large to squeeze
out, it finally forced its way through the mesh, dicing itself in
the process. The fragments hung in the air for a moment, then
miraculously fitted back together again. It began to descend
slowly, as if being lowered on an unseen wire. Its wings were
a mass of shifting colours which you felt you couldn't have

identified even if they'd remained still. The face was more human than butterfly, but its pinched, refined features inspired neither terror nor awe: it reminded you of Doc's expression when medical science had to confess itself baffled, yet again. This time there was no announcement: even Dad – although he knew everything about everything – couldn't name this one. But you could: from the time before speech you remembered and shouted – 'MRRLYMBRXBRX!' – as it settled on your chest and its iridescent wings enfolded your breaking heart.